A FOREVER FAMILY FOR THE ARMY DOC

BY
MEREDITH WEBBER

MILLS & BOON

First published in Great Britain 2017
By Mills & Boon, an imprint of HarperCollins*Publishers*
1 London Bridge Street, London, SE1 9GF

Large Print edition 2017

© 2017 Meredith Webber

ISBN: 978-0-263-06717-0

Printed and bound in Great Britain
by CPI Antony Rowe, Chippenham, Wiltshire

Meredith Webber lives on the sunny Gold Coast in Queensland, Australia, but takes regular trips west into the Outback, fossicking for gold or opal. These breaks in the beautiful and sometimes cruel red earth country provide her with an escape from the writing desk and a chance for her mind to roam free—not to mention getting some much needed exercise. They also supply the kernels of so many stories it's hard for her to stop writing!

Books by Meredith Webber

Mills & Boon Medical Romance

Wildfire Island Docs

The Man She Could Never Forget
A Sheikh to Capture Her Heart

Date with a Surgeon Prince
The Accidental Daddy
The Sheikh Doctor's Bride
The One Man to Heal Her

Visit the Author Profile page
at millsandboon.co.uk for more titles.

When my sister and brother-in-law
discovered they were unable to have
children they began adopting babies and
fostering older children, eventually adopting
six of them. The family they blended
together became very special—not only to
each other but to our wider family—and
brought fun and joy and laughter to all our
lives. This particular sister has been
my greatest support as a writer, and the
first reader of all my books, so to Jenny,
and all her family, this book
and those that follow it are for you.

**Praise for
Meredith Webber**

'The romance is emotional, passionate, and
does not appear to be forced as everything
happens gradually and naturally. The
author's fans and everyone who loves
Sheikh romance are gonna love this one.'
—*Harlequin Junkie* on
The Sheikh Doctor's Bride

'What's the problem?'

'Well, at the risk of sounding embarrassingly ridiculous, I'd like you to understand it's just dinner…not a date.'

Mac's eyes twinkled—and her stomach churned.

'I don't date, you see,' Izzy added, hoping to stop the churning with practicality. 'Well, not at the moment.'

'So dinner…not a date. That's okay.'

The smile playing around his words only added to the stomach-churning!

She sighed again, shrugged, and finally said, 'I can't be late home.'

And if he thought she hadn't noticed the satisfied expression on his face as she finally agreed he was wrong.

Used to getting his own way, was he?

A sure sign this was a man to be wary of.

Dear Reader,

In this book you'll meet Izzy, a foster child brought up by an extraordinary couple who have opened their home and their hearts to waifs and strays, fostering many children over a long period of time.

The house is quiet now, the children all grown up, though Izzy remains living in The Old Nunnery with her foster parents and daughter Nikki. But because of the love they received from their foster parents, Hallie and Pop Halliday, the children are all close, and in the next three books you'll meet more of them—Lila, Stephen and Marty—and follow their lives and their loves as they meet the people who will help them create their own families.

These stories—Lila's in particular—have been in my head for a long time, and somehow this seemed the right time to tell them. I hope you enjoy meeting 'the Halliday Mob', as they were always known around town, and following their lives as they seek families of their very own.

Meredith Webber

CHAPTER ONE

IZZY PACED HERSELF on the run along the coastal path, which, right now, bordered a small sheltered beach. Ahead, the path rose high over headland cliffs, and further on it wound through coastal scrub. A truly beautiful part of the world—the place she loved, the place she belonged.

She'd been working nights, so this early-morning run was in the nature of a reward. A little treat before returning to her real world—making sure Nikki was ready for the start of the new term, catching up with her parents to get the latest family news, walking the dogs across the lush paddocks around the house—relaxing!

Nikki!

Her daughter would be thirteen next month—thirteen going on thirty—sensible, loving, doing well at school. So why was there always a little knot of worry tucked beneath Izzy's sternum where Nikki was concerned?

Izzy stopped—well, jogged on the spot—peering down onto the beach where an unidentifiable lump of something lay just beyond the lapping water.

Too big to be a body, she told the lurch in her stomach, but best she check.

Scrambling down over lumpy rocks from the path to the sandy beach, she caught a glimpse of movement up ahead.

Someone else heading towards the unknown object?

Or someone leaving the—

No! It was definitely too big for a body; besides, the movement had now resolved into a person, tall, dark-haired—lots of dark hair—definitely heading for the lump.

Izzy was the first to reach what was now apparent as a beached mammal, and knelt beside it, speaking quietly, touching it gently—a baby whale? Surely it must be because dolphins were a different shape, sleeker, their faces pointed, beaked…

Although the sun was not yet high in the sky, the animal's skin was hot. Izzy ripped off her T-shirt, dunked it in the waves and spread it over the animal's back.

'Good idea,' a deep voice said. 'I've a towel in my pack, I'll get that.'

He'd turned and was gone before Izzy could get a good look at him, nothing but an impression of a very unkempt man with a lot of facial hair and plenty more in a tangled mess all over his head.

'Bring something like a bottle or a cup if you've got one, and clean water, too.'

She yelled the order after him then returned to studying the animal, trying to remember things she'd learned when she and Nikki had visited Sea World some years ago.

Sea mammals usually stranded themselves on their side.

Tick!

This one certainly had.

The stranger returned.

'Porpoise,' he said in an authoritative voice.

'You think? I thought maybe baby whale.'

A shout of laughter made her look up, and up, to the tousled-haired man standing above her.

'Whale calves are three times the size of this fellow and weigh a ton or more.'

'Know-it-all,' Izzy muttered to herself, but as the man had dunked his towel in the water and was efficiently covering the animal she could hardly keep arguing with him.

And why *was* she arguing?

Did it matter?

'I think the first thing is to get it onto its belly.'

Bit late now to tell him she'd already thought of that.

'But the fresh water?'

Ha, something she knew that he didn't!

Deep inside she wondered at the petty thoughts flashing through her head but hopefully he wouldn't have noticed the momentary pause before she answered.

'Just pour a little over each eye, like where

he'd have an eyebrow, so it will run down. I seem to remember you need to keep the eyes moist but—'

'The salt gets encrusted on them if you use sea water,' he finished for her, smiling, so white teeth flashed in the mess of dark hair.

And something gave a tiny tug in the pit of Izzy's stomach…

No! Not that! No way!

Carefully he poured water to a point above first one eye, then the other, allowing the water to run down over both eyes.

'I'm Mac,' he said, screwing the lid back on the bottle to preserve the rest of the water.

'Izzy,' Izzy replied, lifting her hand towards his so they shook above the body of what was apparently a porpoise. 'We'll have to roll him this way, towards the sea, to get him on his belly and I think if we dig a hole along this side, he might turn easily.'

'You've done this before?' Mac asked, joining Izzy on the seaward side of the animal, and digging into the sand.

'Nope, but I once went to a lecture about beached mammals. Big ones you shouldn't roll because you can break their ribs, and, oh, you should keep the tail and flippers and this fin on the back wet because they cool themselves through these thinner bits of their body.'

Mac, who'd brought a billycan as well as the bottle of water, began filling it and tipping it carefully onto the fins and tail while Izzy kept digging, focused on what she was doing so the tremor of—what? Awareness?—that tickled through her body when Mac settled beside her again, scraping sand away, almost passed unnoticed.

Almost!

What malign fate had brought him to this precise spot at this exact moment in time? Mac wondered as he knelt far too close to the half-naked woman and pulled sand away from the stranded animal.

A three-week trek down the coast path had been an opportunity to clear his head and prepare himself for the new job that lay ahead—

literally ahead, for this particular section of the coastal path ended at Wetherby, not far from Wetherby District Hospital, currently awaiting its new director.

'Director' was a glorified title when the hospital, from what he'd learned, only boasted two doctors, with a private practice of four GPs in support—

'I think he's tilting this way.'

He glanced towards the speaker, who was completely oblivious to the effect she was having on his libido. She was kind of golden—like he imagined a sprite might be. She had golden skin, reddish-gold hair pulled ruthlessly back into a knot at the back of her head, but already escaping its confinement with damp little corkscrew curls flopping around her face. And golden eyes—well, probably brown, but with golden glints in them...

Better to think of the whole of her than individual bits, like the soft breasts, encased in a barely-there bikini top that brushed his arm as they dug—

He stood up, too aggravated by his wayward thoughts—not to mention the apparent return of his libido—to remain beside her.

'I'll lift the towel and shirt off it so we can replace them when it rolls,' he said, and congratulated himself on sounding practical and efficient.

'Good idea,' the sprite said, stopping her digging and scraping for a moment to smile up at him.

Oh, for Pete's sake, she had a dimple...

Fortunately for his sanity, the porpoise rolled into the hole they'd dug and now lay, snug on its belly, the rising tide sending wavelets splashing onto it.

The sprite had leapt away just in time, but she'd caught the full brunt of the splash, so water and sand were now splattered across her skin as she danced up and down in delight, clapping her hands and telling the uncaring animal how clever he was.

'Why do you assume it's a male?' Mac demanded, his reaction to the sight of her capering happiness making the words come out grouchier than he'd intended.

Golden eyes lifted to his.

'Honestly,' she said, a smile barely hidden on her lips, 'do you think a girl porpoise would be stupid enough to get into a fix like this?'

'Hmmph!'

He couldn't recall ever making a 'hmmph' noise before but that was definitely how it came out, but it was time to be practical, not argue over male versus female in the stupidity stakes. He'd certainly been the stupid one in his marriage, assuming it had meant things like love and fidelity on both sides...

Annoyed by the thought, he concentrated on the porpoise.

'What do we do next?'

Izzy studied the still stranded animal. At least it was right way up now, but was she keeping her eyes on it, so she didn't have to look at the man—Mac?

She'd been so delighted when their plan had worked, she'd looked up at him to share the success—straight into the bluest eyes she had ever seen. Right there, deep in the tangled mess of dark hair, was a pair of truly breathtaking blue eyes. She was pretty sure her heart *hadn't* stood still, even for an instant, but it sure had seemed like it…

Think about the porpoise!

'Maybe if we dig a trench, kind of extending our hole towards the sea, he might be able to slide forward as the tide rises.'

'Or perhaps we should get help,' the man with the blue eyes said, giving the impression he was done with the animal rescue business.

Or maybe he was just being practical.

'We're three kilometres from town and I don't have a phone—do you?'

He looked put out as he shook his head, as if admitting he didn't have a phone was some kind of weakness, but who in their right mind would want to carry a phone on a wilderness walk? There were small fishing and holiday villages along the route and anyone walking it was obliged to report each day's destination so a search could be mounted if the walker didn't turn up. And at this time of the year there'd be other people on the path—

She looked up towards it—hopefully...

No people right now.

'So, it's up to us,' she said, hoping he'd stay so there'd be an 'us'. 'I don't suppose you're carrying a sleeping bag?'

'A sleeping bag?'

He seemed confused so she added quickly, 'Thing you sleep in—the nights have been cool, I thought you might—'

'I *do* know what a sleeping bag is,' he growled, 'I just can't see why you're asking.'

Grouchy, huh?

'For a sling,' she explained, although the bemusement on his face suggested he still wasn't with her. 'Can you get it?' she asked, very politely, and smiling as she spoke because she needed this man's help and didn't want to upset him any more than she already had.

'We'll try to slip it under him,' she explained. 'We probably should have done it before he rolled but it's too late now, so we'll just have to build a little pool for him. I don't think we could lift him with the sleeping bag, but once the water rises and takes some of the weight, we'll be able to guide him into deeper water.'

'You want me to put my sleeping bag into the water for this animal?'

The disbelief in his voice stopped all thoughts of politeness.

'Oh, stop complaining and go get it. This part of the track ends at Wetherby. I'll buy you a new sleeping bag there.'

He didn't move for a moment, simply looking at her and shaking his head, as if she, not the stranded porpoise, was the problem.

Muttering something under his breath—something that could have been about bossy women—he turned and strode away, long, strong legs eating up the distance back to the track.

Izzy realised she was staring after him, shook *her* head in turn, and returned to digging with renewed determination.

Better by far than thinking of the blue eyes or

strong legs or the fact that the rest of him, now his T-shirt was wet and clung to a very well-developed chest, wasn't too bad either.

Aware that he was behaving like a loutish imbecile, Mac returned to his already diminished pack and pulled out his sleeping bag, unrolling and unzipping it so it was ready when he reached the water.

Her idea was a good one—he should have thought of it himself.

Was he annoyed because he hadn't?

Or because of his inexplicable awareness of the woman who *had*?

Wasn't he done with that kind of attraction?

Not with women in general—he had several good women friends, some of whom, from time to time, he had taken to bed.

Until that had become awkward—more than physical attraction creeping in—though not on his side.

And the one thing he'd learned from his marriage was that physical attraction was dangerous. It messed with a man's head, leading him to make rash decisions.

And wasn't his head holding enough mess already? The Iraq posting, then finding out about his wife and *her* physical attractions…

Ex-wife!

He shook his head to free it of the past and studied the animal as he approached, determined to take control of this situation.

Wasn't that what ED specialists did?

'I'm deepening the hole—not easy because the sand just washes back in with the next wave but I think if we persist we can do it,' the woman, Izzy, said. 'Do you mind wetting his eyes again?'

So much for taking charge!

But as the tide rose and the water in their porpoise paddling pool grew deeper, he forgot about messy heads and wars and women, determined now to get this creature back into the deeper water where it belonged. He dug until his arms ached, pushing the sleeping bag beneath the heavy body, reaching for Izzy's fingers, grasping towards his from the other side.

By the time the water in the hole was knee deep they had their sleeping bag sling in place, each holding one side, lifting as the waves came in and easing the docile creature inch by inch into deeper water.

'Look, he's floating now,' Izzy said, and Mac was surprised to realise the weight had gone from their sling.

'You're right,' he said, feeling a surge of relief for the animal. 'But just keep the bag underneath him. We need to roll him back and forth so he gets the feel of his body moving in the water. Well, I think that's the idea. I just know when you catch, tag, and release a big fish, you have to ease it back and forth in the water until it swims away.'

He pushed at the huge body and Izzy pushed back, the pair of them moving into deeper and deeper water until, with a splash of his tail, the rescued animal took off, diving beneath the surface and appearing, after an anxious few minutes, further out to sea.

'He's gone! We did it—we did it!' Izzy yelled,

leaping towards Mac and hugging him so the sloppy, wet sleeping bag she was still holding wrapped around him like a straitjacket and he sank beneath the waves.

But once untangled and in shallower water, he returned the hug, the success of their endeavour breaking the reserve of strangers.

He was beginning to enjoy the armful of woman and wet sleeping bag when Izzy eased away, hauling the sleeping bag out of the water and attempting to fold it.

'I don't usually hug str—' she began, then frowned as if something far more important had entered her head.

'Oh, I do hope he doesn't come back,' she said anxiously. 'I hope the rest of the pod are somewhere out there looking for him and he can find them. Do you know that when a whole pod is beached, and rescued, they try to let them all go at once so they can look after each other?'

Well, that got us over the awkwardness of the 'stranger hug'.

He'd have liked to reply, *Not our problem*, but

now she'd mentioned it, he did feel a little anxious that the porpoise—*their* porpoise—would be all right.

Nonsense—he wasn't even certain porpoises swam in pods, and probably neither was she. The job was done and he needed to resume his walk—without his sleeping bag and without drinking water.

Alone?

'I don't suppose you'd like to walk with me as far as Wetherby, or as far along the track as you're going?'

She looked up at him and he noticed surprise in the gold-flecked eyes.

Noticed it because he'd felt it himself, even as he'd asked the question. Wasn't he off women?

Taking a sabbatical from all the emotional demands of a male-female relationship?

Not that it mattered because she was already dismissing the idea.

'Oh, no,' she was saying—far too quickly, really. 'I have to run. I'm just off nights and I've got to check my daughter's ready for school on

Monday and my sister's up from Sydney for the weekend, and I think my brother might be in town—'

'Okay, okay!' he said, holding up his hands in surrender, then he smiled at the embarrassment in her face, and added, 'Although in future you might like to remember something my mother once told me. Never give more than one excuse. More than one and it sounds as if you're making them up on the spot.'

'I *was* not! It's all true.'

Indignation coloured her cheeks and she turned to go, before swinging back to face him.

'There's a fresh water tap just a few hundred metres along the track; you can refill your bottle there.'

After which she really did go, practically sprinting away from him along the track—

For about twenty paces.

'Oh, the sleeping bag,' she said, pointing to the wet, red lump on the beach. 'You can't carry it wet, so hang it on a tree. I'll be back this way in a day or two and collect it so it's not littering the track, and if you tell me where you'll be staying I'll get you a new one.'

Izzy was only too aware that most of her parting conversation with the stranger had been a blather of words that barely made sense, but she *did* need to get back, or at least away from this stranger so she could sort out just what it was about him that disturbed her.

Had to be more than blue eyes and a hunky body—*had* to be!

'I won't be needing the sleeping bag.'

The shouted words were cool, uninterested, so she muttered a heartfelt, 'Good,' and turned away again, breaking stride only to yell belated thanks over her shoulder. Duty done, she took off again at a fast jog, hoping she looked efficient and professional, instead of desperate to get away.

By the time she slowed to cool down before reaching the car park, she'd decided that the silly connection she'd felt towards the man had been nothing more than the combined effects of night duty and gratitude that there had been someone to help her with the porpoise.

Which, hopefully, would not re-beach himself the moment they were out of sight!

Mac resumed his walk with a lighter pack.

But vague dissatisfaction disturbed the pleasure he'd been experiencing for the past three weeks. Maybe because his solitude had been broken by his interaction with the woman, and it had been the solitude he'd prized most. It was something that had been hard to come by in the army, even when his regiment had returned from overseas missions and he'd been working in the barracks.

Strange that it had been the togetherness of army life, the company of other wives and somewhat forced camaraderie, that had appealed to Lauren—right up to his first posting overseas.

'But you're a doctor, not a soldier,' she'd protested, although she'd seen other medical friends sent abroad. 'What will happen to me if you die?'

He could probably have handled it better than promising not to die, which he didn't on his first mission. But by the second time he was posted to Afghanistan she'd stopped believing—stopped believing in him, and in their marriage—stopped believing in love, she told him later, while explaining that the excitement of an affair gave her a far bigger thrill than marriage could ever provide.

On top of the disaster that had been his second deployment, this news had simply numbed him, somehow removing personal emotion from his life. He knew this didn't show, and he had continued to be a competent—probably more than competent—caring doctor, a cheerful companion in the officers' mess and a dutiful son to both his parents and whichever spouses they happened to have in their lives at the time.

He'd always been reasonably sure that his parents' divorce, when he was seven, hadn't particularly affected him. He'd seen both regularly, lived with both at various times, got on well with his half-siblings, and had even helped them, at different times, when their particular set of parents had divorced. Walking the coastal path, he'd had time to reflect and had realised that perhaps it had been back then that he'd learned to shut his emotions away—tuck them into something like a memory box and get on with his life.

Had this shut him away, prevented him from seeing and understanding what had probably been Lauren's very real fear that first time he'd been sent abroad?

She'd contacted him, Lauren, when she'd heard he was back this time—an email to which he hadn't replied.

He'd wondered if the thrills she'd spoken of had palled, but found he didn't want to know—definitely didn't want to find out. In fact, their brief courtship and three-year marriage seemed more like some fiction he'd read long ago than actual reality.

A dream—or maybe a nightmare…

Not wanting his thoughts to slide back into the past where there were memories far worse than that particular nightmare, he shut the lid on his memory box and turned his thoughts to what lay ahead.

Inevitably, to the golden girl—woman—who'd popped into his life like a genie from a bottle, then jogged right back out again.

She must live in Wetherby, he realised, but the seaside town and surrounding area had a population of close to ten thousand, probably double that in holiday time.

It was hardly likely they'd run into each other...

And he'd be far too busy getting used to his new position, getting to know his colleagues and learning his way around the hospital and town to be dallying with some golden sprite.

Besides which, she had a child to get ready for school so was probably married, although he *had* checked and she didn't wear a ring.

Not that people did these days, not all the time, and there were plenty of couples who never married, and women, and men, too, he supposed, who had a child but weren't necessarily in a relationship.

But she *had* a child, and even if she wasn't partnered, he was reasonably certain that women with children would—and should—be looking for commitment, for security, in a relationship.

Not that he did relationships.

He was more into dallying, and since he'd been a single man again, the only dalliances he'd had were with women who felt as he did, women who were happy with a mutually enjoyable affair without any expectation of commitment on either side.

The path had wound its way to the top of a small rise and he halted, more to stop his rambling, idiotic thoughts than to look at the view.

But the view was worth looking at, the restless ocean stretching out to the horizon, blue and green in places, fringed with white where the surf curled before rolling up the beach.

Off the next headland he could see surfers sitting on their boards, waiting for the next good wave, and beyond that what must be the outskirts of the town.

Wetherby!

CHAPTER TWO

THE KITCHEN TABLE at the Halliday house could have seated twenty people quite comfortably, but Izzy and her sister Lila were under orders to set it for eight.

'I thought it was just us—how did we get to eight?' Izzy asked, as she obediently laid placemats while Lila added cutlery.

'Uncle Marty's coming and he'll probably have a new girlfriend,' Nikki, who was arranging a bowl of flowers for the centre of the table, volunteered.

'But that's you and me, two, and Lila, Hallie and Pop, five, then Marty and presumably his latest flirt, that's seven.'

'Plus the new doctor from the hospital. As chairman of the hospital board it seemed only right I get to know him,' the woman her foster children all called Hallie explained.

'She's matchmaking again,' Lila whispered to Izzy.

'Hopefully for you, not me,' Izzy retorted.

'But Lila doesn't live here,' Nikki pointed out. 'And, anyway, Mum, he might be The One.'

Izzy groaned. Thirteen-year-olds—*nearly* thirteen-year-olds—shouldn't be acting as marriage managers for their mothers!

'Now, don't start that again. I am perfectly happy with my single state, besides which he's the new doc and I'll be working with him, and while some people seem to manage to combine their work and social lives, it's always been a disaster for me.'

'It was only a disaster once,' Hallie reminded her, 'and that was probably my fault. He seemed like such a nice man when the board interviewed him. How was I to know he had two ex-wives he didn't happen to mention?'

'Two ex-wives and a jealous lover who damned near shot our Izzy.'

They all turned towards the back door and chorused Marty's name as he spoke. Nikki was first into his arms for a hug.

But Izzy hung back, shuddering at the memory of that ill-fated relationship, only looking up when Marty added, 'Okay, I'm home and it's great to see you all but just stand back, girls, because I found this bloke out in the garden, looking a little lost, and apparently he's come for dinner. Hallie's latest stray, I'd say, the new doc in town. Says his name's Mac.'

Izzy could feel her face heating while her body went stiff with shock. A long drawn out *no-o-o-o* was screaming somewhere inside her, while her hitherto reliable heart was beating out a little tattoo that had more to do with how the stranger looked than who he was.

Clean-shaven, with his long shaggy hair trimmed and slicked neatly back, his blue eyes framed by dark arched brows, he was possibly the most attractive man she'd ever seen.

Any woman's body would react to him, she

told herself, glancing at Lila to see if she was similarly struck.

But, no, her beautiful, dark-haired, doe-eyed sister was shaking hands with the man called Mac and asking where he'd come from, where he'd trained, doctor-to-doctor questions.

Not that Mac had time to answer them, for Hallie had taken charge and was introducing him to the family.

'Marty you've met—he doesn't live here, just arrives from time to time, though usually not alone...'

Hallie frowned and looked around as if realising for the first time that Marty hadn't brought a woman.

'I took Cindy straight upstairs,' he explained. 'She wanted a shower before dinner, then I went out to see Pop in the shed and met Mac on the way back.'

'Ah,' Hallie said, nodding as if the world was now back in its rightful place. 'So, Mac—you do like to be called Mac, don't you? Isn't that what you said at the interview?'

The poor bewildered man nodded, and before Hallie could go off on another tangent—something they were all only too used to—Marty stepped in.

'Mac, the smallest of the women in the room is Nikki, and the redhead cowering in the corner is her mother, Izzy. It's not your fault that the last hospital director had a mad ex-lover who tried to shoot Izzy.'

Marty waved his arm.

'Come on over, Iz, and say hello to your new boss.'

'We've already met,' Izzy said bluntly, her anger at Marty for singling her out overcoming all her weird reactions to Mac.

'And I'm Lila.'

Bless her! She'd read the tension in the room, had probably felt it emanating in waves from Izzy, and had stepped in to defuse things.

Now she was doing doctor talk again with the newcomer, smoothing over the earlier awkwardness and giving Izzy time to recover.

* * *

Mac tried to make sense of the place and people around him. He'd been directed to walk up the hill from the hospital and the only place on the hill was a big, old, stone-built building that looked as if it could house the hospital as well as all the staff.

He'd walked around it, wondering if the chairman of the hospital board might have a real house hidden somewhere behind it, and had ended up in a huge vegetable garden.

The man called Marty had rescued him, leading him into the old building through a cave-like back entrance and directly into a kitchen where, amidst what seemed like a dozen chattering women, stood his sprite. She had clothes on now, stretch jeans that hugged her legs and lower body and a diminutive top that showed a flash of golden skin at her waist when she moved.

Mrs Halliday he recognised, and the young girl with long golden-brown hair—okay, that was the daughter—while the real beauty of the room, the exotic dark-haired, black-eyed Lila, was finding it hard to hold his attention so his replies to her questions were vague and disjointed.

The sprite rescued him.

'This is the man I was telling you about,' she said to the room at large. 'The man who helped me with the porpoise.'

After which she finally turned her attention to him.

'Sorry about the chaos here tonight, Mac, but with—'

'With your sister up from Sydney, and your brother might be home...yes, I know,' he teased.

He saw the colour rise in her cheeks, but the flash of fire in her eyes suggested anger rather than embarrassment.

Bloody man! Izzy muttered inwardly. Now the whole family was looking at her.

Waiting for her famous temper to flare up?

No way! She would *not* react to this man's teasing. Bad enough her body was reacting to his presence, sending messages along her nerves and excitement through her blood. If this kept up she'd have to leave—town, that is—given that a distracted nurse was no help to anyone.

But Nikki—school…

Pop saved her from total, and quite ridiculous, panic by appearing through the kitchen door with a long, and remarkably dangerous-looking spear in his hand.

It stopped both the conversation and the sizzle in her blood.

'This's the best I can do, Nik,' he said, passing the lethal weapon to Izzy's daughter. 'I don't know if the aboriginals in this area made ceremonial markings on their spears but old Dan at the caravan park will know. You can ask him, and he'll show you what it needs.'

'Put that away right now!' Izzy ordered as Nikki began to caper around the room, flourishing the spear dangerously close to several humans.

Nikki disappeared, Hallie introduced Mac to Pop, she and Lila finished setting the table, and peace reigned, if only momentarily, in the Halliday kitchen.

Pop was explaining to Mac the project Nikki would be doing when school resumed, and why she needed a spear.

'I've made so much stuff for so many kids over the years,' he added. 'Izzy, was it you who was the robot? That was probably my most ingenious design, although I did go through a lot of aluminium foil.'

Any minute now he was going to dig out the old photos and she'd be squirming with embarrassment all night!

'Okay, dinner is ready.'

Hallie saved the day this time. She set the roasted leg of lamb on the table and handed Pop the carving knife and fork, Lila brought over dishes filled with crisply roasted potatoes and sticky baked pumpkin, while Izzy did her bit, taking the jugs of gravy from the warming drawer in the big oven and setting them on the table.

'Right!' Hallie said. 'Guest of honour—that's you, Mac—at the head of the table. Izzy, you'll be working with him so you might as well get to know a bit about him. You sit on one side and Lila on the other, and no descriptions of operations of any sort, please, Lila. Pop, you sit next to Lila, and then Nikki, and on the other side Marty and Cindy, and I'll sit at the end because—'

'Because you have to get up and down to get things,' the family chorused, and Izzy began to relax.

This was home, this was family, this was where she was safe, so who cared if her body found Mac whoever he was—did he *have* a last name?—attractive? Of course she'd felt attraction before—although not for quite a while, now she thought about it.

'Are you going to sit?'

Heat crept up her neck and with her hair piled haphazardly on top of her head, the wretched man would see it! How was she to know he'd hold her chair for her?

She thumped down in the seat, too quickly for him to guide it into place, pulled it in herself and turned to offer a brusque thank you. She met the blue of his eyes and felt herself drowning.

This wasn't attraction, this was madness.

'So, why Wetherby?'

Lila saved her again, asking the question that had been in Izzy's mind, only hers had been phrased more as 'Why the hell Wetherby?'.

Now he was smiling at Lila—well, what man didn't smile at Lila?—and the kind of dark voice she remembered from the beach was explaining in short, fairly innocuous sound bites: army doctor, Middle East on and off over the last few years—

'—so when I decided to get out of the service I looked for somewhere green, and close to the surf, yet small enough to be peaceful.'

'Well, it's certainly that—I'm guessing a month here and you'll be bored to tears,' Cindy told him.

'Hey, Cindy, this is my home!' Marty protested.

'And this is only the second time you've been here, Cindy, and then only for a night,' Nikki pointed out.

'Are all small-town people as defensive as

Wetherbyans?' Mac murmured to Izzy, who felt the heat of his body radiating towards her and the breath of his words brush against her skin so all she could do was look blankly at him.

'Of course,' Lila said briskly, and although she'd once again saved the day, she was also studying Izzy closely. Probably trying to work out what was happening.

As if I know, Izzy thought desperately, passing the potatoes to their guest, while Lila piled slices of meat from the platter Pop had filled onto Mac's plate.

Mac took the offerings of vegetables as they arrived and passed them on, poured gravy on his meat, and when his hostess picked up her knife and fork, he began to eat.

He tried to make sense of this family—anything to forget the woman by his side and the effect she was having on him. But how big, blond, blue-eyed Marty could be related to the beautiful Lila, let alone the petite redhead by his side, was beyond him.

'We're foster kids.'

He wasn't sure whether he was more surprised by Izzy speaking to him or the fact that she'd read his thoughts.

'*All* of you?'

'Oh, yes, and there's heaps more of us. It was a nunnery, you see, and Pop bought it for a song when he and Hallie married, and they intended filling it with their own kids, but that didn't happen so they went out and found the strays that careless parents leave behind, or kids whose parents died, in Lila's case. And they gave us all unquestioning love, and stability, and the confidence to be anything we wanted to be. But more than that, they gave us the security of a home, a family.'

'It's true,' Lila said, nodding from his other side.

'And it's been the best thing that happened in all of our lives,' Marty put in, although Hallie was telling them to hush, it was nothing anyone else wouldn't have done.

But for some reason Mac's thoughts had stopped earlier in the conversation so although he'd heard the rest, and been impressed, the question that came out was, 'A nunnery?'

How could these beautiful women be living in a nunnery? Except it wasn't a nunnery, of course it wasn't, it was just that his brain wasn't working too well. There was nothing immodest about the sprite's clothing, but from where he was sitting he could see the tops of the soft roundness of her breasts, and blood that should have been feeding his brain was elsewhere.

'It was cheap,' the man they all called Pop offered. 'And not that hard to knock two or three of the little cells together into decent-sized bedrooms.'

'You're a carpenter? Builder?'

Pop smiled and shook his head.

'Truckie—mainly long haul. I've taught all the kids to drive trucks.'

'I'm learning now,' Nikki announced, adding, rather to Mac's relief, 'Though only in the paddocks behind the house at the moment.'

The talk turned to the animals kept in the paddocks—did Mac ride? That was Nikki. Hallie mentioned the vegetable garden—'Feel free to help yourself to any vegetable…we always have far too many!'—and with the simple, delicious meal, and the general chat, Mac found himself relaxing in the midst of this strange family.

'You've family yourself, Mac?' Pop asked.

'Parents, of course,' he said. 'Though I don't see much of them. The army, you know—you never know from one day to the next where you'll be.'

He didn't add that their regular divorces and remarriages had dulled any filial emotion he'd ever felt for them.

'Married?'

This time the question came from the beautiful Lila and he didn't miss the wink she sent to Izzy.

Best to get that sorted once and for all, and quickly.

'Was once,' he replied, forcing himself to speak normally, although what felt like a very unsubtle third degree had his temper rising.

'And once was more than enough,' he added, to underline the point.

He glanced at Izzy, who was blushing furiously, and realised the questions weren't so much for him but to tease her.

Marty put a stop to it.

'Enough!' he said, directing the word at Lila. 'Pop asked a normal, everyday question, but all you're doing, Lila, is teasing Izzy.'

He turned to Mac.

'Izzy had an unfortunate experience with a doctor we had here a few years ago and it's become a bit of a family joke.'

The shrill tone of a mobile phone broke up the conversation, and it was Marty who pulled one from his pocket, glancing at it and moving away.

'Work. I'll probably have to go,' he explained as he moved into a small room off the kitchen.

'Marty's a pilot on the rescue helicopter,' Lila explained, as the whole family turned anxious eyes towards the small room.

He returned briskly, grabbing a jacket from the back of his chair.

'Got to go! Cindy, you coming or staying? If you're coming there's no time to get your stuff.'

Cindy, too, pushed back her chair.

'Coming,' she said.

The pair had barely left the room when another mobile sounded, and, having been free of its tyranny for three weeks, it took Mac a moment to realise it was his.

He glanced at the message on the screen before he, too, stood up.

'Looks like I'm starting work early. I'm sorry, Mrs Halliday. The meal, what I managed to eat of it, was wonderful.'

'Wait, I'll come with you,' the sprite announced.

'I know the way.'

He didn't really snap, it just came out a bit sharp, images of the tops of her soft breasts still lingering in his head.

'Sure, but you only arrived in town this morning so I doubt you know your way around the hospital. Hallie might have given you the basic tour, but if it's an emergency—and it will be if Marty's flying someone in—then you need the best help you can get, and that's me.'

She paused, then added with a teasing smile, 'So, lucky you!'

She couldn't possibly have known what he was thinking—not possibly, but it was obvious she intended coming with him as she rushed around the table kissing Hallie, Pop, Nikki and Lila, before linking her arm through his and practically dragging him out the door.

Escaping?

It certainly seemed that way as she led him headlong down the hill to the small hospital.

'But aren't you just off night duty?'

Good, he'd not only remembered something she'd said this morning, but had also managed a question, so his brain must be back in gear.

'Yes, but in case you didn't notice there was a certain amount of conspiracy stuff going on around that table tonight.'

'Conspiracy?'

He didn't want to admit he'd been more than slightly distracted by his neighbour at the table.

'Never mind,' Izzy said. 'Silly family stuff! I was just glad to get away.'

She moved a little further from him now she had him out of the house.

Sitting next to him, conscious of every movement of his body, had been torture, especially since she'd noticed the silky hairs on his forearms.

Dark, silky hairs…

Mesmerising dark silky hairs…

She shook her head, glad of the darkness so he didn't see her shaking loose her thoughts.

They were going to work and this was actually a good opportunity to see if she could detach herself from the idiotic attraction and concentrate solely on whatever they had to get done.

Never in her twenty-six years with the Hallidays had she been diverted from the sheer gluttonous enjoyment of one of Hallie's roast dinners, yet there she'd been, her fork toying with a piece of pumpkin as she'd wondered if his arms would feel as silky as they looked.

'But you *have* just come off night duty?' Mac asked, successfully getting her mind off silky hairs—though only just…

'Yes, but I've had a good sleep today. It's why I jog. The steady pace seems to get rid of any leftover work tension and I can sleep like a baby.'

'Some babies don't sleep all that well,' Mac muttered.

What babies did he know?

Not that it mattered...

'We can go in this way,' she told him, leading him to the kitchen door at the rear of the building. 'We've only eleven patients at the moment with another seven in the nursing home at the back, so there'll be two registered nurses and two aides on duty in the main hospital, with another RN on call. Actually, there should be one of the local GPs on call, but there's a wedding...'

She led him down a short corridor, waving to a woman sitting at a curved desk in a room to the left.

'That's Abby,' she told him. 'Abby, Mac, Mac, Abby.'

'Good thing you had your phone on,' Abby told him. 'I wouldn't have known where to find you otherwise. I know you haven't officially started work but there's been an RTA on the highway, helicopter will bring in one patient for stabilisation and onward transport, and there are two ambulances also on the way.'

A patient requiring stabilisation was a tough introduction, but Mac was intrigued.

'And how do you get this information? Know to be prepared?'

He'd asked the question into the air between her and Abby, so Izzy answered him.

'First on scene is almost always police. They radio for ambulance support, a paramedic with the ambulance team assesses the injured and organises everything until the patients are safely removed.'

'He can order a helicopter?' Mac asked.

'Providing one can land,' Izzy responded. 'And Marty can land just about anywhere. Roads are great if they're flat and straight, but around here it's been dairy country since for ever, and there are fields close to the roads even in the hills.'

Izzy was leading him towards the large room that was their 'emergency department', as she explained. The room had a desk, curtains that could be drawn to allow privacy for patients and on the far side, three small rooms.

'The first one is the resus room,' Izzy told him. 'Next to it is a quiet room for mental health patients who sometimes find other people disconcerting, then a kind of all-purpose room, used for everything from resus to upset kids, to talking quietly to relatives when necessary.'

Mac heard a hitch in her voice and knew that talking to relatives—usually with grim news—wasn't one of her favourite things. In a small town, a death would probably be someone she knew...

He wanted to touch her shoulder, say he was sorry, but why?

An excuse to touch her?

To feel that golden skin?

Fortunately, while totally irrational and unmedical thoughts flashed through his mind he heard the *whup, whup, whup* of the helicopter.

Not a big army helicopter carrying injured troops—a smaller chopper, light, one patient.

He was fine, but as sweat broke out on his fore-head he wondered why he hadn't considered res-cue helicopters when he'd chosen Wetherby.

Because he'd thought it was too small?

Or because he'd doubted the noise of the little dragonfly helicopters he'd encounter in civilian life would affect him?

'You okay?'

He shook his head, then realised she'd prob-ably take it as a negative reply, so he said, 'Of course,' far too loudly and followed her out the door, presumably to meet their patient.

The rotors were still moving when a crewman ducked out to open the door wider so they could access the stretcher. Marty appeared from the front cabin to help and Mac was left to follow behind as his patient was rushed with admirable efficiency into the hospital.

Following behind, in the lights that surrounded the landing circle, he could see the patient was in a neck brace and secured onto a long spine board, with padded red supports preventing any head movement. One arm was in a temporary splint, and a tourniquet controlled blood loss from a messy wound on his left leg.

Mac's mind was on procedure, automatically listing what had to be done before the patient was transferred on to a major trauma centre.

'No obvious skull fracture,' the paramedic reported, 'but the GCS was three.'

So, some brain damage! A subdural haematoma with blood collecting inside the skull and causing pressure on the brain?

A CT scan would assess head injury, but would moving him for the scan cause more complications?

This was a patient with spine and head secured and moving on to a major hospital.

Leave the CT scan to them!

Intubation?

Definitely!

A young woman, presumably the paramedic, was using a manual resuscitator to help his breathing.

'The paramedic is intubation trained,' Izzy explained, somehow picking up on his thoughts once again, 'and I know the literature is divided about whether or not to intubate at the scene, but if we're doing the main stabilisation here, the paramedics tend not to intubate as that way they get the patients to us faster.'

Mac nodded. The patient's worst enemy, with severe trauma, was time. The sooner he or she had specialised help, the better the outcome.

So, intubation first, Izzy already checking for any obstruction in the mouth, before passing Mac what he needed for rapid sequence intubation. While he checked the tube was in place, she attached it to the ventilator.

The medical personnel from the helicopter were assisting, one taking blood for testing, the other setting up for an ECG.

'We coordinate our rosters,' Izzy explained as she set up the portable X-ray machine. 'Ambulance, helicopter and hospital, so we always have emergency-trained personnel to assist in a crisis. These two both work at Braxton Hospital when they're not rostered on ambulance or helicopter duty. The helicopter is based at Braxton, an hour and a half away, but the patient was brought here for stabilisation because we're closer.'

Mac wanted to ask why the helicopter pilot was in Wetherby if he was on call, but the screen was in place, the picture showing a shadow that suggested a subdural haematoma and, anyway, he had other things to worry about.

Do a CT scan to be sure?

It meant moving the patient to the radiography room, maybe doing further damage to his spine—

No time!

Mac had already decided he'd have to drill a small hole into the patient's skull and insert a catheter to drain off some blood to relieve the pressure before he could be sent on.

Apparently Izzy had also read the situation correctly and had already shaved and prepped the area of scalp the shadow indicated.

The two paramedics—Mac had decided that's what they must be—had been making notes of all the findings, although all the information would also go directly into the computer. Mac knew the notes would travel with the patient in case of computer glitches.

'Are you okay in helicopters? Did Hallie ask you that?' The gold-flecked eyes were fixed on his face as Izzy asked the questions.

'Practically never out of one,' he told her as he carefully drilled through the patient's skull. 'Why?'

He sounded confident but Izzy was sure he'd gone pale and sweaty when the helicopter had come in.

'Well,' she said, 'another statistic shows better outcomes for serious trauma patients if a physician travels with them. I can stay here and Roger—have you even met our other resident doctor, Roger Grey?—he'll come if I need him. Would you be okay with going along?'

She paused, watching for any hint of a reaction, but Mac's attention was on the delicate job of inserting a catheter into the wound he'd created.

That done, he looked up at her, his eyes fixed

on a point somewhere above her head so she couldn't read any reaction in them.

'Of course,' he said, but so shortly, so abruptly she guessed he'd rather poke a needle in his eye. 'We'll start a drip, and make sure there's saline, swabs and dressings available on the chopper. I'll look at his leg on the way.'

She went off to check, returning in time for Mac to give the order to return the patient to the chopper. However, a grim set to the new doctor's face made her wonder just what horrors he had seen in the helicopters that were used to ferry casualties in war zones.

A wailing ambulance siren recalled her to the other casualties coming in. Megan, the most experienced of the two paramedics, had given up her place in the helicopter for Mac and stayed at the hospital to help with the incoming patients.

There were three, none too serious, but two needing limbs set and the other slightly concussed. Izzy and Megan began the initial assessment, GCS and ECG, palpated skulls for signs of injury, set up drips with analgesia. One by one they were wheeled through to the radiography room for X-rays, and for the concussion patient a CT scan, Izzy blessing the radiography course she'd completed.

It was painstaking work, but needed to be completed swiftly in case some major problem showed up, so time passed without them realising that dawn was breaking outside the hospital, the sun rising majestically out of the ocean.

They were studying the films of the second of the limb injuries, a compound fracture of the ankle, when they heard the helicopter returning.

'That's your lift home,' Izzy told Megan. 'And I think you should take Mr Anderson back to Braxton with you. That ankle will need pins and plating, and you've got an orthopod on tap up there.'

'Good idea. Of course we'll take him. I'll get Marty and Pete in to give a hand loading him.'

Izzy started on the paperwork for admitting the other two patients, one for observation, the other to have further X-rays then a temporary cast fitted on his leg, which would keep the bone stable until the swelling went down and a firmer cast could be used.

'And now we're all done, here comes the cavalry.' Megan nodded to the door where Roger Grey had appeared, accompanied by two of the day-shift nurses.

'Big night, do you need a hug?' Roger said, heading for Izzy with every intention of providing one.

She ducked away. Not that there was anything remotely sexual or untoward in Roger's hugs—he was just a touchy-feely kind of man, and there were often times when a member of the staff appreciated a quick hug.

But ducking away had her backing into someone else—someone who'd come in through the patient entrance, someone with a rock-solid body who steadied her with his hands, holding her in such a way she could see those dark silky hairs...

Moving hurriedly—escaping, really—she made the introductions, gave Roger a brief précis of what they'd already done for the two new patients, explained the third would go to Braxton, then, as exhaustion suddenly struck her, she turned towards the cloakroom. There'd be a bikini, shirt, shoes and socks in her locker. She would run off the tension of the night, then swim, before heading home to sleep.

She peeled off the scrubs she'd been wearing since the ambulances had come in and threw them into the bin by the door—the opening door.

Mac's head poked around it.

'Sorry,' he said, though in bra and pants she was quite respectable. 'I wondered if you were going for a run. It's definitely what I need and we'd look silly running separately along the path.'

She'd have liked to say she was taking the path south but that would sound petty; besides, she wanted to collect the sleeping bag.

So she nodded, in spite of knowing that she was making a rash decision.

'I imagine you'll have to go home and change. I'll wait by your gate.'

CHAPTER THREE

I'LL WAIT BY your gate!

How stupid could she be?

This man, Mac, was causing her enough problems without her agreeing to go jogging with him—actually making arrangements to be *with* him instead of as far away from him as possible, which would have been the really sensible decision.

Although they'd be colleagues so she couldn't escape him forever.

She began some routine stretching so she wouldn't have to think about him—well, not as much…

He emerged in shorts and a faded T-shirt, his hair loose and tangled again, hanging just long enough to hide his ears.

Her body reacted with the little flutters and zings, but she was getting used to them now.

Nearly!

'Sorry to keep you waiting, and sorry to barge in on your run as well, but there were things I wanted to know.'

He brushed against her as he shut the gate, and, yes, the hairs were just as silky as they looked, and, no, she was *not* going to touch them...

'Such as?' she said instead.

'If your brother was on duty last night, shouldn't he have been in Braxton where the helicopter is based?'

They were walking briskly through the town and fortunately it was too early for many of the locals to be around.

'He has his own—his own helicopter, I mean. He can be back in Braxton as quickly as if he'd driven from his house there to the hospital. The paramedics load any extras he might need while his crewmate checks the machine. All he really does is get in and fly the thing, although he was a trained paramedic as well as the pilot.'

She paused, wanting to ask her own question about helicopters, but realised it was probably far too personal.

So she stuck with Marty.

'Even when he was young he had a passion for them. Pop made him a little model one that had some string around the rotor stem and you wound it up then pulled and the helicopter took off. But most of the time he just ran around with it in the air, making helicopter noises, diving, and rising, and chasing the rest of us.'

They'd reached the track and set out in a slow jog.

'You were a happy family, then?' he asked, turning to look at her as he asked the question, his eyes studying her face.

Looking for a lie?

'Very,' she said firmly. 'Oh, we had our fights like any family and there were always kids who found it hard to fit in.'

She faltered, paused, looked out to sea before adding, 'Some of them had been so traumatised, so badly abused, they hated being happy, I guess.'

Mac nodded. You couldn't get through training as a doctor without seeing the horrific things people could do to one another—could do to children. At least, that was what he'd thought until he'd gone to war.

'Hallie and Pop must be remarkable people,' he said, forcing his mind back to the present as they resumed their jog, speeding up slightly.

'They are,' Izzy agreed, and the simple confirmation, the love in her voice, told him far more than the words.

They jogged in silence, and he breathed in the sea air and marvelled at the might of the waves crashing against the cliffs, the beauty in the scraggly, wind-twisted trees along the path, the little cove…their porpoise cove?

'The helicopter bothered you last night?'

He'd been so lost in his contemplation of the scene—concentrating on the details of the beauty around him to avoid his reactions to the woman beside him—that the question startled him.

He didn't have to answer it, he decided, but within a minute realised his companion—colleague, as he should be thinking of her—wasn't so easily silenced.

'Just the sound of it coming in made you go pale, yet you agreed to accompany the patient to the city.'

She was stating a fact, not asking a question, so now he didn't have to…

Except…

Except he wanted to!

For some reason, in this beautiful place, with this woman he barely knew by his side, he *did* want to talk about it.

'It wasn't fear so much as memory,' he said, stopping to look out to sea while he found the words.

Not the words for the unimaginable horror—no words could cover that—but enough words to explain, to her and to himself.

'On my last tour one crashed—not a medical evac chopper but a big Chinook, carrying troops. One guy died and the others were badly injured.

Getting them out of there was surreal, like living a nightmare. We weren't in much danger, weren't under direct attack, but putting men who'd been through what they'd been through into another bird, well, some of them just couldn't handle it.'

A hand slid into his and small fingers squeezed his.

'Were you able to sedate them?'

He nodded, then admitted, 'Only some.'

She removed her hand, stepped away to look more closely at him, folded her arms—to stop her hand straying again?—and shook her head.

'Well, I think given that experience, plus all the other things you've seen, you were remarkably brave going off last night.'

He had to smile at her fierce defence of him, a man she barely knew, but smiling at her brought a smile to her face, too, and the dimple peeped from her cheek.

And there was no way he couldn't touch it—just reach out and brush his forefinger against it.

She lifted *her* hand. To smack his away? But, no, all she did was brush her fingers across his forearm, then she beckoned with her head so once again they began to jog.

But the touches, unexpected yet somehow intimate, had changed something between them. It was acknowledgement certainly, but was it also acceptance of the attraction that had inexplicably sprung up between them, right back when they'd first met?

Or was he being fanciful?

Did she feel it or was her touch nothing more than a casual gesture?

Did it matter when he'd decided he didn't do attraction any more?

And he certainly didn't dally with colleagues...

He shook his head—he didn't do fanciful thinking either. Somewhere along the coast path to Wetherby he'd lost his common sense.

But glancing towards her, her strides lengthening now, the golden limbs moving with such grace, he felt a tightening in his gut, *and* in his groin if he was honest—

Tricky when they worked together.

Especially tricky when he knew the danger of physical attraction…

He lengthened his own stride, catching up and keeping pace with her, but they were beyond casual conversation now; it was a sprint, an unspoken challenge, and when she muttered, 'To the she-oak,' in laboured tones, he understood the challenge.

They sprinted, and male pride made sure he won, although she wasn't far behind, collapsing against the rough bark of the tree, fighting for her breath, while he was bent, hands on knees, dragging air into his depleted lungs.

'Well, if that doesn't help us sleep, nothing will,' Izzy finally had breath enough to say.

Mac, still bent, turned his head towards her.

'That was torture. I'm a walker, not a runner.'

But he was smiling as he spoke, and Izzy knew for certain she was lost. It had been bad enough when he'd touched her cheek and she'd reacted by feeling those silky hairs, but bent over, smiling up at her—a teasing smile—she understood that whatever it was she was feeling it was mutual.

And dangerous!

Especially now, when getting involved with a man was the last thing she needed—well, wanted...

And as for attraction, that was just a fleeting thing, and too easily confused with love, and love would be downright impossible just now.

Ignoring it seemed the best option, so she stood up straight, pulled off her shirt, kicked off her runners, and headed for the beach.

'It's a safe swimming spot if you don't go out too far, where there could be rips and undertows.'

Mac had straightened up and now he looked around.

'Isn't this our beach?'

Dear heaven, surely they weren't going to have an 'our' beach! Not yet, not already—this was moving far too fast and she wasn't even sure what 'this' was...

Although she knew for sure she didn't want it.

'No,' she said firmly. 'The porpoise cove—' no *our beach* from her! '—was the last one we passed, and someone had already removed your sleeping bag.'

But he'd stripped the T-shirt off his chest, and the sight of his upper body, a six-pack, no less, left her too breathless to say more.

She raced down the beach and dived beneath the first wave, the cold water providing a cooling balm to her overheated body.

Not that he was going to let it go, she realised as he, too, dived in and emerged beside her.

'A cold swim is as good as a cold shower, I guess,' he said, smiling down at her, and while she was deciding that the man was just a flirt who went for any woman within reach and she should steer very clear of him, he tucked a strand of hair back behind her ears, then licked his fingers.

'Mmm…salty,' he murmured, before diving beneath the water again.

Well, that was weird, but didn't it prove that he was *definitely* a flirt who went for any woman within reach, and she *definitely* should steer clear of him?

More chilled by her thoughts than the water, she headed for the beach, crossed the rocks that guarded it, then pulled on her shirt. She'd carry her runners back to the fresh-water tap and clean her feet of sand before putting them on.

Mac was still in the water, swimming strongly back and forth across the little cove, but heeding her warning not to go too far out.

Realising he couldn't stay there for ever, Mac reluctantly left the water, walked up the beach, and along the path to join Izzy at the tap. That touch on her errant curl had been a mistake, and given that he *was* attracted to the woman, such touches were to be avoided in the future.

They barely knew each other, and he really should be putting all his efforts into getting this, his first civilian job, sorted. He'd managed the emergency situation the previous evening satisfactorily—even managed the helicopter flight—but responding to an emergency was automatic.

It was the rest of the job he had to get on top of, things like who did what, and when, and where.

There'd be rosters and staff duty statements and daily, weekly and monthly targets—all the bumf so beloved of bureaucrats everywhere, not only those in the army.

He eyed the woman standing waiting for him. It was a wonder she hadn't jogged away, but as she hadn't…

Keep your distance? suggested his sensible self. But surely the thought in his head would count as sensible!

'I don't officially start work until tomorrow, but you obviously know your way around the hospital, so I wondered if, after we've both had a sleep, you'd mind showing me around and telling me how things work and who's who, and how the GPs fit in and—'

'Who's good and who isn't, who's lazy and who's great?'

'No, no, I'm sure they're all great but it's more about—I don't know. I've an appointment with the hospital manager tomorrow morning but I have a feeling that will be all facts and figures and paperwork, not patients and staff and—'

He halted suddenly, mainly because those brown-gold eyes were fixed on his face.

Studying him or drinking in every silly word he was muttering?

'More to get a feel for the place,' she offered politely, and he laughed, not so much at the mock politeness but that she'd picked up on what he'd been trying to ask.

Not that she'd said yes…

'Four o'clock?' she suggested, and he felt a surge of pleasure—well, he was pretty sure it was just pleasure.

'Great! Maybe we could even have dinner afterwards—you can show me the best places to eat in town.'

Had he gone too far? She hesitated.

She had a daughter.

A partner as well?

'Okay,' she said, 'but I can't be late home. Nikki goes back to school tomorrow and she can twist Hallie and Pop around her little finger and they'll let her stay up as late as she likes.'

She paused then added, with a smile, 'They never let *us* stay up late before a school day!'

And in spite of the complaint, Mac read the love for the people who'd brought her up in her voice and saw it shining in her eyes.

Was she out of her mind?

Her body was already attracted to this man, so what would happen if she got to know him better?

Did he read her hesitation in her agreement that he asked, 'What's the problem?'

'Well, at the risk of sounding embarrassingly ridiculous, I'd like you to understand it's just dinner, not a date.'

His eyes twinkled—and her stomach churned.

'I don't date, you see,' she added, hoping to stop the churning with practicality. 'Well, not at the moment.'

'So dinner, not a date, that's okay.' A smile

playing around the words only added to the stomach churning!

'Although at the risk of *my* sounding ridiculous, why don't you date? Not that I expected it to be. A date, you know—'

Of course he wouldn't—a guy who looked like him could have any woman he wanted, so why waste time with a scrawny redhead, especially one encumbered with a daughter?

So she'd made a complete fool of herself even mentioning dates.

And had a question to answer!

She looked at him and sighed.

'Long story but I'll definitely take you over the hospital this afternoon.'

'And tell me the long story over dinner!' he said firmly. 'Stories are good over dinner, and it's *just* dinner!'

She sighed again, shrugged, and finally said, 'We'll see, but I still can't be late home.'

And if he thought she hadn't noticed the satisfied expression on his face as she finally agreed, he'd be wrong.

Used to getting his own way, was he?

A sure sign this was a man to be wary of.

The hospital tour turned out to be fun. Mac insisted on meeting all the patients, and had sat and talked to the men and women in the nursing-home section. It didn't take long for one of the men to winkle out the information that Dr Macpherson—'Please call me Mac'—was an ex-military man and as two of the residents had seen service in Vietnam, topics of conversation weren't hard to find.

The women were equally impressed by the fact that Mac's grandmother had belonged to the Country Women's Association, and the conversation shifted to scones.

'Izzy here makes beautiful lemonade scones,' someone said, and Mac's eyebrows rose.

'Really? Well, those I'll have to try,' he said. 'But right now I've persuaded her to have dinner with me so she can tell me all about Wetherby, and the hospital, and probably you lot!'

One of the men chuckled.

'Is a good gossip all you want?' one of the men teased, and the rest laughed, although as she and Mac departed, her cheeks pink with embarrassment, another of the residents called out, 'Now you take care of her, mind. She's a special girl, our Izzy.'

Izzy expected Mac to laugh it off, but instead he walked slowly away, turning his head from time to time, as if to study her.

Searching for her specialness?

As if!

Interesting, Mac decided.

Were all the patients as protective of this one nurse as the nursing-home residents obviously were?

And what had someone said at that chaotic introduction to the Halliday family?

Something about someone trying to shoot her?

'As you left me to choose where to go for dinner, I decided the Surf Club. They have the best dining room in town as far as position goes, right by the beach, looking out over the ocean.'

Practical—she was practical, he decided, half listening while still following his train of thought.

'It only does basic stuff, like steak and fish and usually a roast, but it's quality food and well cooked.'

She didn't turn towards him as she spoke and he sensed she was still a bit put out about the man's remark.

He walked beside her, through quiet streets towards the beach, avoiding the centre of town, such as it was.

'Are there many restaurants in town?'

Her pace slowed and now she turned to look at him.

'You've really been thrust in at the deep end,' she said. 'You've barely had time to settle into the house, let alone see the town.'

'My own fault,' he told her, hoping his voice was steadier than he was feeling, because a ray of light from the streetlamp was lighting up the side of her face, and the curls he now realised would always escape her attempts to tame them, glowed red-gold against the paler gold skin of her cheeks.

Or was it the line of her profile that had started attraction stirring again? A clean line, smooth forehead, straight nose and soft pink lips above a chin that, while not too obvious, suggested determination.

What would it take to break her determination not to date?

He swung back towards the sea.

What on earth was he thinking?

His head was still a mess, and anger over Lauren's behaviour still simmered somewhere deep inside.

He knew the anger was more to do with humiliation than infidelity, an army base being such a hotbed of gossip, but that didn't make it easier.

And marriage definitely wasn't on the cards—not again. But dating—provided they both knew that was all it was—was different. Dating, and a dalliance, on a short-term basis, could be fun.

Except he didn't dally with colleagues.

Or with women who had children…

Izzy was talking about the town—had been for some minutes, he suspected—while his mind bounced between the present and the past.

'So recently we've had all kinds of new places spring up—offering Paleo and vegan food, as well as more exotic fare from the Middle East and North Africa. It's a result of people making what they call a "hill change" and coming to live in the country outside the town, growing weird and wonderful new fruit and vegetables, and refugees from other countries settling here.'

Fortunately, they'd reached the beach and there, on the right, was the Surf Club. But out in front was the ocean, and above it a nearly full moon, marking a path of silver out to the horizon.

'Magical, isn't it?' Izzy breathed, stopping to admire the view.

'Magical indeed,' Mac agreed, but he was including the moonlit woman beside him in his reply.

Maybe he was bewitched!

Didn't witches have red hair?

Or maybe black—

'Come on, we can see it from the restaurant,' the witch was saying, and he turned and followed her, dragging his thoughts from the mystical to the practical.

All the business of his discharge from the army, getting a job, the three-week walk—it had been a while since he'd been with a woman, that's all it was...

She should have chosen the Moroccan restaurant in the back street of the town, Izzy decided as the young waiter showed them to a table on the front veranda. The view out over the ocean, the white curl of the waves crawling up the curving beach, the surf crashing on the rocky headlands made it far too romantic a backdrop for what was 'just dinner'.

Studying the menu, deciding what to eat, these were helpful, practical things to get romance out of her head.

She didn't date!

Not at the moment anyway...

Not until...

Fortunately Mac seemed similarly intent on the offerings and choices so conversation was avoided until the waiter departed, leaving them a bottle of iced water and taking their orders with him.

'So,' Mac said, as the waiter disappeared, 'why don't you date?'

She frowned at him.

'Is that really any of your business?'

'Nope!' A cheeky smile accompanied the word and undid the little scrap of common sense she'd managed to regain with the decisions about eating.

'But you did say you'd tell me over dinner,' he reminded her.

She wasn't sure she *had* said any such thing, but she'd already realised this was a very persistent man, so she might as well get it over with.

'Nikki isn't mine,' she began, then realised that hadn't come out the way she'd meant it to. 'Well, she is but she wasn't.'

This was getting worse and heat was rising in her traitorous cheeks.

'I mean, I'm not her birth mother. Her birth mother was one of our sisters. She came to live with us when she was seven and not even the love Hallie and Pop gave so freely could make up for the horrific abuse she'd suffered as a young child. It was as if there was something broken inside her, too broken to ever be fixed...'

She'd been playing with her fork as she spoke but now glanced up at Mac, worried she'd begun this story in the wrong place and was boring him.

But his expression held interest, and also understanding, so, encouraged by a slight nod of his head, she ploughed on.

'Nikki was drug addicted when she was born. Her mother died soon after, asking me to care for her baby. As if she needed to ask—the baby was family. But drug-addicted babies are sick and fractious and Nikki demanded so much attention that any relationship was out of the question. In fact, I gave up my pre-med course and spent two years just looking after Nikki. Hallie and Pop were wonderful, of course, but she needed...'

The words dried up, and a lump the size of Ayers Rock had formed in her throat as she remembered that time.

'A mother,' Mac said quietly. 'I can understand that.'

Izzy nodded.

'Anyway, she got better, and life settled down. I decided I'd do nursing—I had credits from the pre-med course—and Hallie and Pop were happy to babysit.'

'So then you were too busy studying to date?'

Izzy returned the smile that accompanied his words, although exchanging smiles was dangerous when even a smile could knot her stomach.

'Go on,' he encouraged, and she shrugged.

'There's not much more to it,' she said.

'Nikki's nearly thirteen years old,' he pointed out.

This time it was a sigh, not a shrug—a huge sigh!

'You know, I'd never thought about it before I had Nikki, but it's darned hard for a single mother to have normal relationships. Not only because you have to cancel if the child throws a fever, or starts coughing, or falls over and needs stitches, but because you start to worry about introducing strange men into her life.'

'*Strange* men?'

Another smile and this time a tweak along Izzy's nerves!

'I mean different men—not family. And what happens if she gets to know and like one of them, then the relationship falls apart and he's gone? There was no way I was going to bring a string of men into Nikki's life—not that I've ever had a string of men—but somehow it seemed easier not to bother.'

'So you never dated?'

Blue eyes dared her not to answer.

'Are you always this persistent?' she demanded, 'But if you must know, yes, I did—well, occasionally. Then—'

'Then? And, yes, I am always this persistent.'

Izzy had to smile, although memories of her last disastrous almost-relationship made her shiver.

'Someone with a gun?'

She looked up into the blue eyes.

'How did you—? Oh, dinner last night—bloody Marty opening his big mouth. Yes, another doctor, a couple of years ago—since him we've had agency doctors. Nikki was ten, and somehow I had decided I needed a man in my life—well, in both our lives. She'd been asking questions about her father but I had no answers, then I began to worry what might happen if she *did* have a father.'

She put down the fork, straightened it carefully, fiddled with the knife, then continued, 'Well, of course she'd have a father, everyone does, but what if he suddenly appeared from nowhere? What if he took her?'

Mac heard what sounded very like panic in her voice and reached out to cover her restless fingers with his hand.

'I thought if she already had a father—a stepfather, but someone she might come to consider a father—then—'

'She'd be safer?'

Mac was rewarded with a blinding smile, although he suspected the shine in her eyes was from unshed tears.

'Exactly,' she said, her voice stronger now. 'I mean, Nikki's always had male role models in her life with Pop and all the brothers, but I kept thinking maybe if we were a family—a mother, father and daughter—she'd be safer.'

Mac could see a kind of weird logic in this, but he was caught up in the story and wanted to know more.

'So?' he prompted.

The gold-brown eyes met his, clear now but dubious, then she shrugged and continued.

'The man—the new doctor—came. Hallie matchmaking, I suspect. Anyway, he asked me out, and we…we got on well. We'd dated exactly four times when his ex-girlfriend turned up. She threatened Nikki as well as me.'

Now her eyes held memories of the horror and he tightened his hold on her hand, while anger at a man he'd never met gripped his gut.

'So, the man you went out with thinking it

might end up being a good thing for Nikki ended up putting you both in danger?'

Her eyes widened with surprise and a small smile replaced the tension around her lips.

'That's exactly how I felt! Talk about an idiot! Anyway, it put me off all thoughts of relationships, at least until she's away at university or travelling overseas.'

Their meals arrived, barramundi for him and lamb cutlets for Izzy, and tackling the tantalising offerings brought the conversation to a halt.

But Mac couldn't help considering the things he'd just learned as he ate his fish—delicious fish. Izzy was busy cutting the meat from her cutlets so he could watch her as he ate.

Not obtrusively, but glances, checking out that she was as attractive as he'd first thought, but also wondering what else was going on inside her head, because she certainly hadn't told him *all* the not-dating story.

Not that he was interested in dating either— well, not a colleague anyway. Far too incestuous somehow! Small hospital, small town—very like an army base—far too easy for stories to spread.

And the attraction thing bothered him. He knew he was attracted to her, and suspected it was mutual, but he knew only too well how attraction could blind a man to other facets of the 'attractee's' personality. Hadn't he and Lauren met and married within eight weeks?

And wasn't he determined not to make the same mistake again—the getting-married mistake? Attraction was fine. Short, mutually enjoyable affairs could be fun, although he doubted that would be possible in a town this size.

'The problem was...'

He was so lost in his own thoughts it took a moment to realise Izzy was speaking to him.

Well, who else could she be speaking to?

He lifted his head, raising his eyebrows.

'The problem was?' he repeated.

She sighed, looked out to the ocean for inspiration, before eventually meeting his eyes.

'Losing Nikki!'

He could hear the tears clogging her voice and reached out to touch her lightly on the arm.

Maybe not a good idea as she flinched and drew her arm away, swallowed hard and finally looked at him again.

'She's not legally mine, you see, so for the last few years—since then—I've been trying to adopt her, which isn't easy when I'm not a blood relative, I'm single, no one knows who or where her father is, and the law says both parents have to agree. I don't even have a formal agreement from her mother—all I have is a note on a piece of grubby paper, asking me to look after her.'

Mac felt his gut tighten in empathy for this woman's fears for the child she so obviously loved.

'I'd been vaguely looking into adoption when the other doctor came along and I knew if I was married it would be easier.'

She frowned, but possibly more at her thoughts than at him.

'I thought if it worked—with the doctor— we'd be a family. Not like our big family, though that's essential to both of us, but a kind of regular family…'

'Mother, father, children kind of family?' Mac asked, wanting to tease with the words but sensing she was very serious about this.

'Exactly!' she said, her smile lighting up her face, obviously delighted he'd somehow understood.

Not that he had!

Although he was reasonably sure it was all to do with Nikki and her safety.

Protection in case some drop-kick birth father turned up and wanted to take her away?

'So I went out with him, the other doctor, had those four dates and we got on okay, but then the gun thing happened and—'

He waited, sure there was more.

And there was…

'The woman threatened Nikki as well—the both of us, in the flat—and the thought I might have lost her, well, I went back to pushing the adoption idea. To adopting her as a single parent.'

'But surely in this day and age, adoption isn't all that hard, even for single women.'

Bewitching golden eyes met his.

'Don't kid yourself! Quite apart from the fact that Nikki's father appears to be untraceable, and she has never formally been handed over to the state for adoption, there are formidable background checks on all adoptive parents, on their homes, their friends, their social life.'

'Ah,' Mac said, as the penny dropped. 'So a string of lovers in your life could rule you out?'

'Even one could, because that would show there could be a string in the future and would that be in the child's best interests? Not to mention the invasion of privacy that the one lover might suffer.'

She sighed, then added, 'So...'

'It's easier not to bother,' Mac finished for her.

He considered this for a moment.

'But isn't that hard on you?'

His answer was a brilliant smile.

'Not really,' she said, shaking her head. 'You get out of the way of it, dating I mean, and I have heaps of men in my life with my brothers and their friends and friends at the hospital, so there's always someone who'll take me along to anything that needs a partner. In fact, I'm very happy with my life.'

Hmm, Mac thought, but he didn't say it, although Izzy's story had affected him deeply.

But not deeply enough to stop the attraction?

As if that mattered. If she did get involved with a man, he'd need to be committed both to her and to a future with her—to marriage—and apart from the fact that the helicopter ride had proven to him he wasn't over the effects of PTSD, he'd decided that he was probably genetically unsuited to marriage, given his parents' and his own failures.

And why was he considering marriage at all? It was a first date—well, not even a date…

CHAPTER FOUR

IZZY STARED OUT at the limitless ocean, wondering why on earth she'd told this man—this virtual stranger—things she'd never voiced to anyone, not even Lila.

The family knew she'd talked about a formal adoption, but although they may have guessed, she'd never voiced her fear of losing Nikki.

'Does this happen with all the women you take out to dinner?' she asked, turning back to her companion. 'Do they all pour out their deepest, darkest secrets to you?'

She hoped the words came out lighter than they felt inside her head, because inside her head was a mess, what with having to resist the attraction and then the unguarded conversation, and the totally unnecessary moon over the ocean.

'Not usually on the first d—dinner,' he said,

a smile in the words, eyes twinkling, although he was serious when he added, 'but I do understand how you must feel. I've seen drug-addicted babies before so those first years must have been hell, and having fought for her to stay alive, to be well at the end of the withdrawal time, it would make her extra-special to you.'

'I had good teachers in Hallie and Pop. Most of the kids they took in had problems, some of them horrendous ones, yet they showered us all with love.'

'And you, did you have problems?'

The question was so unexpected, she answered automatically.

'Not really. My mum dumped me on Gran when I was about three—we never quite figured out when—then Gran died when I was six, and after a while in temporary foster homes I was lucky enough to be given to Hallie and Pop.'

'You make is sound like an ideal childhood, which it can't possibly have been.'

He was frowning, but Izzy couldn't help smiling at his words.

'Compared to some it was, and the love we all got from Hallie and Pop made us a happy family and our world a very happy place.'

She checked the moon again—still there— *and* the ocean, silvered in its light, and sighed.

'We should probably go.'

Not that she wanted to, but the scene must have bewitched her and she'd already told Mac far too much about herself. Stay here and who knew what else might come out?

'I suppose we should. Will I see you at the hospital tomorrow?'

Izzy repeated the words in her head. Did he sound as if he wanted to?

Not that it mattered, of course! No dating!

'Not tomorrow. I'm still on days off, and with Nikki back at school it's a chance to do a big spring clean.'

'You do know it's autumn?' he teased, smiling at her again.

One smile, that's all it took to put her heart back into fibrillation! She had to get over this. Every fibre of her being was yelling at her to keep right away from him. He was a dangerous distraction and the less she saw of him the better.

Work would be okay—well, kind of okay—and unavoidable—but she could handle things at work.

'Autumn clean would sound stupid, but spring clean—well, people know what you mean.'

It was such an inane remark she wasn't surprised he raised his eyebrows at her.

But that was better than him smiling.

And he'd pushed back his chair so they were leaving.

Which meant she could get out of there without making an even bigger fool of herself.

She caught up with him at the bar and reminded him it was just dinner and they should go Dutch, but the beautiful surfie chick behind the bar had already taken his credit card and given him a dazzling smile.

He returned the smile with a pretty good one of his own, and Izzy walked away, reminding herself it didn't matter who Mac smiled at, they were colleagues, nothing more.

But that made walking along the esplanade towards the hospital, and Mac's house beside it, very uncomfortable, because the presence of moonlight and rolling surf and the old lighthouse on the hill was a scene for romance, and the presence of Mac's body, so close to hers, was an agonising distraction.

'I was looking at pictures of the old hospital when you were showing me around,' he said. 'I hadn't realised that the nuns had once run the place.'

Well, that tells me there will be no further personal conversation, Izzy realised, *which isn't fair because he now knows far more than I'm comfortable with about me and I know zilch about him.*

'Yes,' she said, playing the game. 'The church used to be the other side of the hospital so the three—church, hospital and doctor's house where you live—formed a curve of the old brick and stone buildings. The church burned down and there was damage to the rear of the hospital so it was all rebuilt, keeping the old façade.

Your house was saved, and although it's been renovated from time to time, it's pretty much as it was when it was built.'

'It's certainly a lovely old building,' Mac confirmed. 'I'm lucky to be able to live in it.'

Tension tightened Izzy's body. This matter-of-fact, almost tourist talk felt wrong after all they'd shared.

Well, after all she'd shared...

Somehow during their dinner—during most of the time they'd spent together—Mac had shown he was a kind and caring man, not a robot mouthing platitudes about old buildings.

It's just attraction, Mac reminded himself, when his determined discussion of the old hospital buildings had failed to distract him from thoughts of the woman by his side.

And she's a colleague...

And she doesn't date, let alone dally—

The stupid thoughts were brought to an abrupt halt as the blare of a horn split the night air, and a roaring sound filled his ears.

Some sixth sense made him grab Izzy and

together they rolled back onto the road, while a massive semi-trailer ploughed straight past where they'd been standing and crashed into the massive fig tree that was a feature of the hospital's grounds.

'Are you all right?' he asked, as he helped Izzy to her feet, steadying her for a moment as tremors of fear, or perhaps relief, ran through them both.

'Fine!' she said, 'But whoever was behind the wheel of that rig isn't.'

But Mac was already on his way, running towards the crushed cab, as staff came hurrying from the hospital.

The driver's-side door was jammed, but he could see the driver slumped sideways in the seat, his hand still on the steering wheel, on the horn that had warned them of danger.

Then Izzy was there, climbing into the cab from the passenger side, gesturing him to join her.

Not altogether easy, as the tree prevented him

from going around the front of the vehicle, and getting around the back would take too long.

He went over the top, using broken branches of the tree to steady himself, sliding off the bonnet and into the cab.

'Faint pulse at first, but I lost it. His feet are trapped,' Izzy said, as she pumped the man's chest, counting her compressions.

'I'm too big to get down there, but I'll do the CPR if you can edge your way in and maybe release them.'

He watched her squirm her way down into the compressed foot space.

'It's no good.'

Her voice was muffled by the sound of the engine.

Engine!

'Can you reach up and turn off the engine?'

The silence was almost more deafening than the noise had been.

'Now, tell me exactly what's holding his feet in place.'

A nurse Mac hadn't met had arrived from the

hospital with a resus bag, and a siren told Mac that help was on the way—hopefully a fire truck with cutting equipment.

'It's the engine block, I'd say—come back with the impact. I can see his feet, just can't budge them.'

Mac's mind flashed through dozens of road accidents he'd seen, some caused by carelessness, others by the dreaded IEDs.

'Try taking off his shoes,' he suggested, as he slipped a mask over the man's nose and mouth while the nurse attached the tube to the small oxygen tank in the bag.

You try taking off his shoes! Izzy wanted to retort, but she could see it was a good idea—just not easy to do. She wriggled and squirmed, finally getting one shoe off the size-twelve foot, and, like magic, the foot was free.

The other was harder, but by now she could hear voices outside the cabin, and knew more help was at hand. Metal shrieked as some kind of tool was used in an attempt to pry the driver's door open, and although the door remained shut there must have been some movement, because now she could reach the other shoe—well, steel-capped boot, in fact—and pulling a boot off was far harder than removing a shoe, something she must remember to tell Mac.

'Who's in there?' she heard someone ask.

'Driver and a nurse,' Mac replied. 'Driver's feet are trapped.'

'Get her out. We have to start cutting and although we've got foam to cover the cab, if there's spilt fuel, the welding torch could still spark a fire.'

'You hear that, Izzy? Out now!'

It was an order, but—

'One minute. Give me one minute,' she said, as fear for the trapped driver gripped her. She grabbed the boot with both hands and gave an almighty tug, crashing backwards into Mac as the boot came off.

Her held her for a moment, then lifted her bodily out of the cab, passing her to a fireman as if she was a weightless bundle of skin and bones. The fireman set her on her feet, grinning as he recognised her.

'Seen you looking better, Iz!' he teased, passing her over to Roger, who was on call for the night.

'You okay?' he asked, and she nodded, easing away from his side so the comforting arm he'd put around her shoulders fell away. Roger's hugs were fine, but if she'd wanted a hug right now it wasn't from him.

Dangerous thoughts!

She walked back towards the crash site, keeping out of the way of the ambos now lifting the driver onto a trolley. Mac was there beside it, keeping the resuscitator tube free from kinks, checking oxygen flow and the rise and fall of the patient's chest.

'Have you brought some kind of curse down on us?' Roger was asking Mac. 'Two nights here and two accidents! We can go months without an emergency!'

Mac shrugged, passed the tube and oxygen

bottle to Roger, then stepped back, looking around, his gaze coming to rest on Izzy.

Remembering the ambo's comments, she realised she should have gone straight home once the cavalry had arrived. Now Mac was going to see her in whatever state she must be in.

And just *why* was that bothering her?

She wasn't interested in Mac.

Attracted to him, yes, but interested?

Definitely not!

'I'll walk you home,' the person in whom she was *not* interested was saying, and although she'd have liked to refuse, her legs were suddenly shaky and the hand that took her firmly by the elbow was comforting.

'Had he had a heart attack, do you think?' she asked, to distract herself from comforting.

'I'd say so.'

'He must have known something was wrong,' Izzy suggested. 'Big rigs don't usually come through town but he was headed for the hospital and he was giving everyone warning that he was on the way. His hand was definitely on the horn.'

She hesitated, then added, 'It could have been Pop! We all keep telling him it's time to retire and he's not driving as much these days, but when you see something like that...'

Mac heard the tremor in her voice and shifted his hand from her elbow to put his arm around her shoulders—comforting her, nothing more.

Although when the fireman had mentioned fire, he'd felt his lungs seize up.

'Thanks,' she said to him when they'd climbed the path behind the hospital and reached the nunnery. 'And thanks for dinner. I'm sorry I talked so much. You know my entire life story and I know nothing more about you.'

It was too dark in the shadow of the building to see the flush of embarrassment he was sure was colouring her cheeks, and he knew, for certain, that he should let things go right there.

So what prompted him to speak again?

To say, 'Well, we could fix that. You could show me one of the other restaurants tomorrow night—and I'd let you pay half to prove it's not a date. I have meetings at the hospital in the morning but if I know anything at all about hospital meetings, mine will probably go on all day and I'll have no time to shop. So, shall we say six o'clock? Helping out a new colleague, nothing more. Please?'

He heard her sigh and held his breath. Though every functioning cell in his brain was telling him he needed to see less of her, not more, he wanted her to come, wanted to get to know more about the woman to whom he was so inexplicably—and inconveniently?—attracted.

'Okay,' she finally agreed, 'six o'clock.'

And with that, she vanished.

Well, she probably hadn't vanished, there was obviously a door somewhere along the wall that he hadn't noticed and certainly couldn't make out in the darkness.

Izzy escaped into the building, heading quietly up to the small suite of rooms that Pop had turned into a flat for her and Nikki. She looked in on her daughter, thankfully sound asleep, then headed for the bathroom, turning on the light and seeing her dirt-streaked face and scratches here and there where she'd obviously rubbed against something.

At least the path home, mostly in the shadow of the nunnery, had been dark so Mac might not have noticed.

Mac might not have noticed?

The question shrieked in her head. She wasn't interested in Mac. It was attraction, nothing more, and right now, with the adoption process under way, the last thing she needed was a man making things difficult.

She stripped off her clothes, showered, and went to bed. In five hours she'd have to be up, getting Nikki organised and off to school.

Life would return to normal, whatever normal was.

Mac woke bathed in sweat and shivering uncontrollably. The nightmares he thought he'd left behind somewhere on the coastal track had returned, possibly because of the near miss he and Izzy had suffered when the big rig had crashed.

He closed his eyes and breathed deeply, murmuring the words he'd adopted as a mantra— 'truthfulness, compassion, forbearance.'

He'd first heard them used at a meditation session his psychologist had suggested he attend, and for some reason they had made sense to him. Now they helped to clear his mind and calm his body so meditation could be followed by dream-free sleep.

Sometimes!

Tonight his mantra didn't work.

Concern over a new job?

He didn't think so.

Regret over the mess his marriage had been because surely Lauren wouldn't have gone looking for excitement if their marriage had been better?

No, he'd been down that track so many times he'd accepted it was just one of those things.

Which left Izzy.

Hearing her story—he'd seen drug-addicted babies and knew just how much they suffered and how big a task it must have been for her to take on—had added admiration for the person she was to the attraction that had sprung between them in the beginning.

But he also understood just how important her daughter was to her, and he had to be careful not to cross any lines that might put Nikki's adoption into danger.

And apart from that, the nightmare had been a reminder that he hadn't fully recovered—another reason not to get involved with an attractive redhead!

Who definitely didn't want a man in her life!

Just now, or any time?

'Get over it, Mac, get back to truthfulness, compassion and forbearance, breathe in, breathe out, breathe...'

Izzy was slipping a casserole into the oven when Nikki returned from school.

'Yum,' her daughter said, sniffing the air in their small flat. 'Chicken Marsala. Pity I'm going out. Sorry, Mum, I forgot to tell you. Shan and I need to work on our new media assignment so I'm sleeping over at her place.'

'The new media assignment you were going to do in the holidays?'

Nikki laughed.

'We *did* make a start—we decided on a topic. Has the rise in the ocean temperature contributed to the increasing number of great white sharks off east coast beaches?'

'That's media, not biology?'

'Oh, Mum, of course it is. What makes the biggest headlines in a newspaper these days? Four people injured in a traffic accident or a surfer bitten by a shark?'

'Shows how much I know,' Izzy said. 'Well, the casserole will do for our dinner tomorrow night, because I'm showing Mac around town tonight and thought we might end up at the new Moroccan place.'

'Mac? Two nights running? You're dating! And another doctor! Oh, Mum!'

Izzy knew she should have kept quiet, but when did she not react to Nikki's teases?

'I am *not* dating the man,' she said firmly, although the disbelief in her daughter's blue eyes suggested it hadn't been firmly enough. 'If and when I decide to go on a date with a man, I will let you know.'

'Well, if and when you do decide, I hope you know not to go too far on a second date—that's coming on too strong, Mum.'

'Coming on too strong?' Izzy growled. 'It is *not* a date and, anyway, who made you an expert?'

'It's in all the magazines, Mum, and people talk about it in online chat rooms—the ones you let me join.'

Izzy smiled. This was an easier conversation—her daughter's grievance that she had limited online options was a common argument. And one in which she'd held the line—so far!

But tonight Nikki wasn't going to air it, flitting away with, 'I've got to change and pack a few things,' and popping her head back into the combined kitchen and living room to say, 'Just check there's no mad ex-lover in his life.'

Cheeky brat! Izzy thought, but she was still smiling, pleased that she could have these conversations with her daughter—pleased Nikki could have them with her.

She knocked on the bathroom door, and opened it a crack.

'Do you want me to run you down to Shan's?' she asked.

'No, Hallie and Pop are going to the restaurant for dinner, so they'll drive me, but thanks.'

Izzy was closing the door when Nikki spoke again.

'Do *they* know about your non-date?'

'Well, no, but that's only because I haven't seen them today. There's no reason not to tell them.'

'Good,' Nikki called after her, 'because everyone in town will know, probably before you get to his house.'

Brat indeed, but she was right.

Izzy sighed. How on earth had she got herself into this situation? *Why* on earth had she said yes? He was a grown man, ex-army, he could find his way around a small town!

So this would be the last time they had a—what?

A rendezvous?

And to ensure he couldn't use the 'no time to shop' excuse again, she'd take the car, and they could do his shopping either before or after dinner.

Which was possibly one of the stupidest ideas she'd ever had, she realised later as she pushed the trolley around the supermarket while he threw in things he wanted.

Too domestic by far!

Too intimate somehow, especially as she kept running into people she knew and having to introduce Mac.

Which was when she realised that shopping together—although they weren't *really* shopping together—made them look like a couple.

She couldn't keep adding 'I'm just pushing the trolley' to the end of every introduction, now, could she?

'What kitchen paper do you use?'

She was so lost in her 'couple' conundrum it took a moment to realise he was talking to her.

'Whatever's on special usually, although I do like it to be three-ply.'

'Kitchen paper comes in different plies?'

'Of course—the more plies, the thicker it is.'

'Well, what do you know?'

Mac was shaking his head, but now searching each pack for the little sign that gave the ply.

And Izzy, looking into the trolley for the first time and seeing the random selection of goods, forgot her worries over how shopping with him would look to the town and began to sort the contents.

'You've not shopped much?'

'Hardly ever,' he admitted. 'Maybe for coffee, or some biscuits for my quarters, but the army does meals rather well.'

'So you can't cook either?' Izzy demanded, and saw the hesitation on his face.

'Maybe just a little—bacon-and-egg sandwich and that kind of thing,' he said. 'But I've bought some books and one of my stepsisters said that if you can read you can cook, because cookbooks have very clear instructions.'

Izzy shook her head.

'So did you read the book before you came shopping? Write down a list of what you might need in order to cook something you'd read in your book?'

Mac grinned at her.

'Books—I bought two, and, yes, I read one of them on the walk and it all seemed easy enough, but I didn't know until you arrived that we were going to shop.'

'Heaven save me from a helpless male,' Izzy muttered. 'Is there any food at all in your house?'

Mac nodded.

'I've got bread, butter, honey, tea bags and coffee, biscuits, and some milk—most of it left over from the walk, although the milk's fresh.'

'Great start! But to even get the basics, we need time and a list, so what say we abandon this trolley and get some dinner? We can make a list of basics while we're eating and come back later.'

CHAPTER FIVE

SOUNDED GOOD TO MAC. Wandering around
the supermarket with Izzy had been a weird
experience, but one he'd found himself enjoying more and more. It felt comfortable—right,
somehow—and it was impossible to drop things
into the trolley without the occasional brush of
skin on skin, which added sizzle to the exercise.

Not that he should be thinking of sizzle—not
with Izzy. She was definitely off limits!

'So, where shall we eat?'

'Do you like Moroccan food?'

They were walking out of the store, and she'd
turned to look at him.

'Love it,' he said, glad for it to be true. 'In fact,
one of the cookbooks I bought was a Moroccan
one because we had a cook at one time whose

family was Moroccan and it was some of the best food I ever tasted in the army.'

She smiled and shook her head.

'Most men would have stuck to steak and sausages—barbeque stuff—but, no, you go for something that a lot of women wouldn't try! At least that will make writing the list easier.'

She was still smiling, and there was something about a smiling sprite that did weird things to his intestines, but he manned up.

'It will?'

'It will,' she confirmed, leading him to the right, along what was obviously the main street in town. 'We'll know what spices to get, and things like dates, and dried apricots, and couscous, and rose water—'

'Rose water? You've got to be kidding!'

This time she laughed, and that felt good—good that he could make her laugh.

But it was treading on very dangerous ground, this being pleased about something so trivial.

Not that making someone laugh was trivial, but it all felt too…

Domestic?

'It's here—not very imaginatively named but great food.'

Izzy pushed through a curtain of glass beads then held them for him to enter the Marrakesh.

He eased past her, careful not to touch—well, not too much—and breathed in the odours of spice and sauces.

'Wonderful!' he said, as Izzy greeted a man who was obviously the owner, dressed in a smart suit with a dazzlingly white shirt.

'This is Hamid,' she said to Mac, and introduced the two of them. 'Hamid's son, Ahmed, is going to be Australia's next great surfing champion. He's still only young, but beating professionals quite regularly in local competitions.'

Hamid waved away the compliment with eloquent hands but his chest had puffed out and Mac knew he was secretly delighted. Once settled at the table, menus in hand, he realised the scope of Moroccan food.

'I might need guidance,' he said.

Izzy glanced up and smiled.

'No menus in the army?'

'Certainly not this size!'

So she explained the different dishes, asked if he wanted something before the main meal.

'Hamid's mezze plate is wonderful, although it's not specifically Moroccan, more a general Arabic dish, with dips and lovely breads, olives and other bits and pieces.'

'Sounds good, and after that I'll have the chicken with prunes and apricots. Apricots seem to grow wild in Afghanistan and there's nothing as wonderful as a fresh one plucked from a tree. We even had them growing in our compound in Iraq.'

Izzy shook her head.

'We see war as such a terrible thing, and I know it is, but the pictures in the media here show things being blown up, or ruined vehicles or buildings, not a soldier reaching up to pluck an apricot from a tree and biting into it. That's so normal!

Mac grinned at her, something she wished he

wouldn't do as grins seemed to make people complicit—as if they shared a secret.

'Actually,' he admitted, 'there's more time than you'd believe for things like apricots. "Hurry up and wait" is an old army saying. Yes, things are unbelievably hectic at times but in between...'

He shrugged, drawing far too much attention to broad shoulders in a blue shirt that stretched across a well-muscled chest.

She closed her eyes momentarily, mainly to banish an image of the chest beneath the shirt. Was there a god or goddess way back in ancient history or maybe a wise woman spirit guide on a tropical island she could call on to banish attraction? Or maybe a spell—some potion she could take...

She couldn't think of any kind of help so opened her eyes to find Hamid had arrived to take their orders.

That part was easy, but sharing a mezze plate meant inevitable touches of fingers. Izzy could feel tension spiralling along her nerves, tightening every sinew.

This had to stop!

She would help him shop, then cut all ties outside work hours. Even at work she could probably avoid him, and surely she was professional enough to handle things when she couldn't.

She was sufficiently distracted that she didn't see Hamid remove the much-depleted mezze plate, but when he returned with the chicken for Mac and a couscous and baked vegetable dish for her, she knew she'd have to pull herself together and make polite conversation.

Or perhaps a list!

A list would be much easier.

She dug a pen from her handbag, pinched a paper serviette from the table next to them and folded it into note-size.

'So,' she said, brightly, 'exactly what do you have in the way of supplies already?'

His eyes narrowed slightly as if maybe he'd guessed she needed a distraction.

'You can eat your dinner first,' he said, spooning food into his mouth. A pause while he chewed and swallowed, then, 'Mine's delicious.'

Izzy obediently ate a few mouthfuls.

'There,' she said, 'now we can both eat and talk. Basics are bread, butter, milk, tea and coffee, which you seem to have covered.'

'The bread's going a bit green.'

'Okay, so bread...'

She wrote it down.

'Now, breakfast—what do you eat for breakfast?'

Mac held up a hand, obviously giving his full attention to his food.

'It's wonderful,' he eventually said. 'Maybe I can persuade Hamid to give me some small containers of this dish and I could have it for breakfast, lunch and dinner.'

'You'd grow to hate it,' Izzy suggested, and he smiled.

Smiles affected her, but it was, she decided, better than the grin.

'Probably,' he admitted. 'What do you have for breakfast?'

'Totally boring,' Izzy told him. 'Cereal, yoghurt, fruit.'

Another smile.

'That would do me. Write it down.'

Izzy sighed.

'You can't possibly be this hopeless,' she grumbled. 'You must know there are choices. There must be hundreds of types of cereals alone, not to mention plain and flavoured yoghurts—'

'And all kinds of fruit,' he finished for her, shaking his head and laughing. 'Don't look so serious. I can make those choices in the shop. I'll just grab something that looks good and if I don't like it, I'll get something different next time.'

She didn't want to smile at him but a laughing Mac was hard to resist. The problem was that smiling at him arrested the laughter and something passed between them—nothing more than a quick clash of gazes—but it worried Izzy more than all the other sensations that being with Mac caused.

'Lunch?'

She spoke firmly, wanting to bring things back

to normal between them. 'A sandwich? Cheese, ham, tomato, lettuce?'

And suddenly he was as decisive as she was.

'Ham and cheese—they'll last longer.'

Mac wasn't sure what had just happened, but something had—something that had been more than attraction—something dangerous, although not darkly so...

He scooped more of his meal onto his spoon and ate in silence, only half listening as Izzy added practical things—dishcloths, soap, washing powder—to his list.

Mac used her concentration on the list to study the woman across the table from him, a little frown drawing her eyebrows together. She wasn't a classic beauty, or even stunningly attractive, yet his body responded to every move she made, and every word she spoke. It was as if they were attached to each other with invisible wires—which was such a ridiculous fantasy he couldn't believe he'd thought it.

He had to get his head straight.

He had to keep things light between them.

He knew her well enough by now to know she wasn't a dallying kind of woman, even without the vulnerability of her position in regard to Nikki's adoption.

And there were still too many dark places in his psyche to think beyond dalliance with any woman.

They finished their meals—and apparently the list—he wiping his plate clean with some thick, fresh-baked bread, though Izzy seemed too distracted to have eaten all of hers.

But she pushed her plate away and said, 'Come on, let's go. You paid last night so it's my turn.'

He protested that she was doing him a favour but she ignored him, handing her credit card to Hamid to stop any further argument.

But back in the supermarket—shopping with her—it seemed dangerous again.

She had to get out of here, Izzy decided. Finish this as quickly as possible and get out—get home. For some obscure reason an ordinary wander around a supermarket was beginning to feel like a date—more like a date than dinner had.

She knew it wasn't, of course, but—

'That should keep you going,' she finally declared, heading resolutely towards the checkouts.

'That's if I can pay for it and don't end up in debtors' prison.'

'What, this little lot?' she teased, waving her hand at the almost full trolley. 'Back when we were young, we'd have Hallie pushing the lead trolley with three or four of us trailing along behind, each with a trolley.'

'The mind boggles,' Mac said, easing Izzy away from the handle and taking over the pushing, his body still close and warm.

'Oh, I need some toothpaste!' She dashed away, grabbing two tubes, although she knew there was plenty at home.

Anything to get away from that warmth—that closeness—that somehow, even when he hadn't been near her, she'd been feeling.

'Throw them in with mine as thanks for all the help, not to mention the lift you're going to give me,' Mac suggested, and rather than argue—and get close again—she threw them in.

Once back at his house, she helped him unload the bags.

'I'll leave you to unpack so you know where you've put everything,' she said, backing towards the door as escape finally beckoned.

'None of this will go off if left for a few minutes, so I'll walk you home.'

'I've got a car,' Izzy reminded him. 'But thanks for the offer.'

'Then I'll walk you to your car,' he said, and did just that, opening the driver's door for her so their heads were close. She met his eyes and knew something was passing between them... like the promise of a kiss that couldn't be...

CHAPTER SIX

IZZY WAS STILL MUTTERING, 'Promise of a kiss, indeed…' to herself when she reported to work the next morning. The walk down from home had been pleasant, dawn breaking, the first rays of the sun peeking from below the horizon.

She loved the town when it was like this, barely awake, and the early shift, beginning at six, was her favourite.

Abby, still on nights, was waiting for her in the ED.

'Ambulance on its way in—four-year-old with febrile convulsions. Little Rhia Watson—Sally and Ben's daughter. I've written down all the handover stuff—it's on the desk—and the other night nurse will do a proper handover to Chloe, who's on with you today—I think an agency nurse is coming for the swing shift.'

The conversation ended as the ambulance pulled up outside, and both women hurried out to meet it.

'She woke up crying in the night,' Sally explained as Ben carried his daughter into the room. 'Her temperature was up so I gave her some children's paracetamol and sponged her down, but nothing seemed to help. We stayed with her, trying to keep her cool, and she drifted off to sleep then about half an hour ago she cried out and when we went in she was all stiff and shaking.'

'I called the ambulance,' Ben added, as he carefully laid his listless daughter on the examination table. 'She'd stopped shaking by the time they got there.'

The ambo was handing over his report to Abby, and although Izzy knew it would have all the details of Rhia's temperature, pulse, and oxygen saturation she knew she'd have to do it all again.

After she'd examined the little girl.

She took Rhia's hand. 'I'm Izzy and I'm a

nurse and I'm going to look after you. Mum and Dad are still here. Now, can you tell me if you're hurting anywhere?'

'My head hurts…and my neck.'

'Get a doctor in here,' Izzy said quietly to Abby. She didn't want to alarm Rhia's parents but with neck pain or stiffness in a child this age there was always the possibility of menin-gococcal.

'Now, I'm just going to look at your tummy, is that okay?'

Dark brown eyes dulled by pain or fatigue looked blankly at her as Izzy checked the little girl's skin for any sign of a rash.

None, but that didn't mean anything at this stage.

'I'd like to give her an antibiotic injection just to be sure,' she said to the parents, who nodded, willing to go along with anything to make their little girl better.

'You're thinking meningococcal?' Mac asked quietly.

He had appeared from nowhere, but had obviously heard her.

'Or not,' Izzy said, 'but we usually start with an antibiotic just in case, then do the tests.'

He nodded, and she went off to get the penicillin while Mac introduced himself to the family and began his examination of their patient.

'Has she been vaccinated against meningococcal?' he asked, and Sally held out her hands in a helpless gesture.

'I think she had a needle for that when she was one but I'd have to check.' Fear brought a quaver to the words. 'Do you think that's what it is?'

Mac reached out and touched Sally's shoulder.

'We don't know but the fever means an infection and starting antibiotics straight away will help no matter what it turns out to be.'

He nodded to Izzy, who told Rhia about the needle, and waited until Ben had lifted his daughter into his arms before swabbing the skin, using deadening lotion, then slowly administering the antibiotic.

Rhia cried, but it was a half-hearted effort, and her listlessness made Izzy fear the worst.

Mac was explaining that he would need to take blood and some cerebrospinal fluid for testing, and Izzy suggested they move to the small room that was sometimes used as a second resus room.

Mac nodded, then smiled down at Rhia.

'Do you mind if *I* carry you instead of Daddy?'

There was no objection so he lifted her and carried her gently into the more private space. Izzy asked Ben to wait and with his help she filled in the admission form before leading him to join the others.

Mac had settled Rhia on a high table and with Izzy's help secured an IV port in their patient's little hand. He handed Izzy a vial of blood to be sent off for testing, then explained to Rhia that he needed her to lie on her side so he could put another needle in her back.

'I'm sorry sweetheart,' he said, smiling at the little girl, 'but we need to find out what's making you sick. I'll do my best not to hurt you.'

But Rhia was beyond caring, she simply stared

at Mac with those big blank eyes, while Sally cried quietly on her husband's shoulder.

So Izzy held their patient curled on her side on the table while Mac numbed the site with local anaesthetic, then inserted the needle to test CSF pressure before withdrawing a sample. Izzy cleaned and covered the site with a dressing before gently rolling Rhia onto her back.

Mac was putting details on the chart, so Izzy labelled and packed the fluid container, added the blood sample to the package and passed it to the courier she had phoned earlier.

'Now we wait,' Mac said quietly, as Rhia's parents moved closer to their daughter, one on either side, holding her hands and talking quietly.

Mac followed Izzy out of the room.

'If it's confirmed as meningococcal we'll have to find out who's been in contact with her for the last week and give them all a dose of clearance antibiotics—starting with her parents. And if it *is* meningococcal there'll be a run on the vaccine. Is it subsidised by the government or will people have to pay for it?'

'If she had the vaccine, and she probably did, it would have been Type C. Since that's been on the free list the most common strain in Australia is B and although there's now a vaccine for it, you have to buy it.'

Mac nodded.

'We'll have to admit her, if only for observation—at least until the test results come back.'

'She could go into the family room, and that way her parents could stay with her. She's an only child and Sally's a stay-at-home mum so she could be here all the time and Ben go to work from here.'

Mac grinned at her.

'Family room, huh? I did wonder why one of the rooms had a double bed.'

Was it the grin or the mention of a double bed that raised Izzy's heart rate?

'It's a very useful room to have,' she said reprovingly. 'Apart from making it easier for hospitalised children to have their parents with them, it's been great for elderly people especially. Imagine being married for sixty years and suddenly your spouse is hospitalised twenty miles away. It's too much to expect them to visit for an hour or two each day.'

Mac's smile was back and with it Izzy's heightened pulse.

'I'm still back at the imagining being married sixty years part—I didn't make it to three.'

'Didn't work out?'

She remembered him saying he'd been married—back at that embarrassing dinner. And something else—that he wouldn't marry again?

His marriage must have been bad.

And the wretch was still smiling.

'I think you'll find in your statistics that something like forty percent of marriages fail.'

'You're wrong, it's one in three marriages fail so that's thirty-three percent,' Izzy muttered, disturbed by the conversation, although she couldn't work out why.

Mac's life, former, present, or future, had nothing to do with her.

Mac watched her walk along the passage that gave entry to the rooms that made up the ward.

He liked the design of the hospital, with an enclosed courtyard garden on the other side of the passage. And along the outside of the patient rooms was a long veranda so those well enough could sit outside, enjoying the sunshine and the view over the town to the ocean.

Halfway down was the nurses' station, well set up with computers, monitors and light boxes. Someone had taken the trouble to make the new hospital, in the damaged part of the old building, into a relaxed and pleasant place for patients, and a great working environment for the staff.

'You're Mac, I believe,' a voice said from behind him, and he turned to greet a young Asian woman, the crisp white coat and the stethoscope slung around her neck a dead giveaway that she was a doctor.

'I'm Aisha Narapathan,' she introduced herself, holding out a slim hand for him to shake. 'I've a patient in Room Fourteen, and I pop in to see her most mornings.'

Mac introduced himself, and smiled.

'You're from the local GP group?'

Aisha nodded.

'We act as on-call doctors when you and Roger are off duty and although our patients are happy with the treatment they get in hospital, I like to check up on them myself. At times when there's been only one doctor employed at the hospital, and we've been rostered on for morning rounds. It might seem a clunky system at first but it works.'

She smiled again, and added, 'Most of the time. You've had a busy weekend, I hear. Normally one of us would have been on call—we cover weekends as well—but Saturday night was our receptionist's wedding and, it being a country town, we were all invited.'

'We managed,' Mac assured her.

'I'm sure you did,' Aisha said. 'With Izzy around, even the most helpless of the contract doctors we've had at the hospital can manage.'

She moved on but not before Mac caught the flash of a bright diamond on the ring finger of her left hand.

Was she the doctor engaged to Roger Grey?

His thought was confirmed when he saw her as she was leaving.

'You must come to dinner one day. Roger and I would love to have you. I'll tell him to arrange it with you.'

An aide arrived with a message. There was a phone call for him in his office.

He headed in that direction, pausing only to say goodbye to Aisha.

Was this job going to turn into a deskbound one? Surely not—and not if the weekend was anything to go on.

But interaction with people—with patients and their relatives—was the part of medicine he enjoyed the most.

The voice on the phone introduced himself as the pathologist at Braxton Hospital.

'I've emailed the results to you but thought it would be good if we spoke.'

He introduced himself, asked the usual questions about where Mac had trained, seeking acquaintances in common, then explained.

'It's meningitis meningococcal for sure. The

bacteria are present in the spinal fluid but none in the blood.'

'Thanks, mate,' Mac said. 'I owe you one for getting it done so quickly.'

But as soon as he'd hung up he wondered if the hospital would have ceftriaxone on hand, or whether he should have ordered some for Braxton.

There were optional drugs, but lately it had been the one of choice for meningococcal attacks on the brain.

He looked up from doodling the name on his desk pad to see Izzy flash past the door.

'Izzy!'

She turned, stopping in the doorway. For the first time he realised just how horrible the dark blue uniform tunic looked on a redhead, although he still felt his groin tighten just looking at her.

'Ceftriaxone?' he asked.

'So it *is* meningitis,' she said, her voice flat with the anxiety she felt for the child. 'We've some in stock. I'll set up a drip.'

'I'll do it,' he said, 'but come with me while I tell Rhia's parents. They'll feel better with someone they know in the room.'

Will they? Izzy wondered, but she accompanied Mac back to the family room, where Mac explained the result.

He did it well, she realised, listening to his explanation of what was happening inside their daughter's body, then moved swiftly on to treatment.

'We've got it early,' he told them. 'You were right to get help immediately she had the seizure. There are good drugs to treat it and we'll start a drip straight away so the antibiotic is going directly into her bloodstream. I'll also give the pair of you antibiotics and later the vaccine.'

He turned his attention to the small patient in the big single bed in the family room.

'I know you're feeling bad right now,' he said, stroking strands of pale brown hair off her face, 'but we're going to get you better.

'She'll be here for a few days, probably longer,' he said quietly to Ben on his way out the door.

'You might want to get some toys she's familiar with and her own pyjamas and a few clothes for her and the pair of you.'

'And books. I'll get books—she loves us reading to her.'

Hmm…Izzy thought to herself when she heard Ben's voice strengthen at the thought of having something to do to help. She knew already that Mac was a good doctor, he'd shown that in the emergencies over the weekend, but he was also a good psychologist.

Or perhaps just a caring man, sensitive to how Ben must have been feeling?

Whatever! She didn't need to be seeing these compassionate sides of him, they would add depth to the silly attraction she was already feeling.

But right now at least she could get away from him—she had a job to do in the pharmacy.

Except he caught up with her on the way and it was hardly a pharmacy, just a room where drugs were kept.

A very small room!

She paused outside the door.

She didn't *have* to go in!

Of course she did, she knew where it was kept.

He'd stopped beside her and she was so conscious of him her skin itched.

This was crazy—there was no other word for it. She'd been attracted to The Rat, as her family now called the last man in her life, but not like this—not as if the attraction was a tangible thing, not only causing responses inside her body but in her skin as well.

'What's the protocol?' she asked, forcing her mind to matters medical, fumbling with her keys to find the right one as if that, and not her disinclination to be in a very small room with him, was the hold-up.

'Seven days' IV for Rhia, in saline, not Ringer's, because it doesn't mix well with anything that has calcium in it. Then we'll have to give antibiotics to any people who've been in close contact with her in the last week, and check all of their statuses as far as vaccination goes. We'll get a list of friends and relations from her parents. Was she at childcare of any kind that you know of?'

Whatever was affecting her couldn't be affecting him that he was being so practical.

She could do practical!

'She's four. She'd be at the local pre-school probably three days a week. I'll get our secretary to phone the director and get a list.'

'Of teachers, too,' Mac reminded her as she finally got the key to fit into the keyhole and unlocked the door of the pharmacy.

They stepped inside together—close—and without turning to face her Mac said, 'I understand your reluctance to be going out with men because of the adoption business, and I know it's bizarre, but I've never felt an attraction like the one I feel for you. I thought maybe if we gave in to it, say for a week or two, it might go away. That's if you feel it, too, of course...'

His voice was only slightly strangled, but Izzy knew any words she said would come out far worse—if at all.

He'd touched her lightly and somehow they

turned to face each other, not touching, not close enough to cause a scandal should anyone walk past, but Izzy could feel the shape of him in her skin, catch the warmth of his breath on her lips.

'You *must* feel it,' he said. 'Something this strong can't be one-sided.

She almost nodded—no way could she deny it. But caution, memory of the last disaster— and somewhere in her head and heart concern for Nikki—held her back.

'The ceftriaxone should be in here,' she said, moving towards a cupboard where she knew the powder was kept. It would be dissolved in the saline solution and dripped slowly into Rhia.

Then Mac was right behind her, peering into the cupboard, examining its contents, taking his cue from her—now totally professional.

'I have had a look inside these cupboards and the refrigerators but, as yet, couldn't put my hand on anything.'

'Which is why you have staff,' Izzy told him, so rattled by his presence she was shaking.

'Staff I can put my hand on?' he teased, touching her lightly on the shoulder. Not *quite* professional!

Was he another Rat or just another touchy person like Roger?

Izzy doubted it—this was something they both felt.

'We can't talk here,' she said desperately, a vial of the yellowish powder in her hand.

'Then later?' he asked, his breath now warming her neck.

'Sometime!' she said, almost shouting, desperate to get out of the room, away from Mac, if only so her body could settle down and her brain regain some thinking power.

He moved away, finding a bag of saline for all he'd said he didn't know his way around.

Izzy glanced at her watch—it had been less than five minutes since they'd left the corridor, yet it had seemed like a lifetime.

But was he right? Could a short—short what? Affair? Liaison?—kill the attraction?

She had no idea but as it was impossible to

think while he was in such close proximity, she chose escape.

'I'll leave you to mix it if that's okay? I've other patients I need to check. They'll be thinking no one cares about them.'

And she fled, although her excuse hadn't been entirely true. Patients in a small hospital knew the staff could become caught up in emergencies and they bore it well, knowing it could be them or one of their loved ones who needed urgent attention next time.

And Mac was probably intuitive enough, from what she'd seen of him, to know it, too.

Was he avoiding her as assiduously as she was avoiding him? Izzy wondered later, when she was sitting in the secretary's room, working out how she could juggle the rosters for the week.

They would need more nursing staff on duty to handle vaccinations and antibiotics for adults and children who'd been in contact with Rhia, and the budget didn't have much wriggle room.

'Here's the list from Sally and Ben. They've included phone numbers where they knew them.'

She looked up to see Mac hovering over her desk, a piece of paper in his hand.

'One of the aides could have delivered that,' she said, disconcerted to have him back in her space when she'd thought she'd escaped.

She'd been looking up at him so saw from a half-smile that he was about to say something silly, then he glanced towards Belle at the desk at the back of the room and must have thought better of it.

Instead he tilted his head to see what she'd been doing. 'Have we enough staff to help out with the vaccinations when people hear about it and start coming in?'

Izzy pointed at the sheet.

'It's a juggling act, but staffing at small hospitals always is so, yes, we'll manage.'

A soft chime told them they had a patient in the ED and the enrolled nurse on duty there needed help.

'I'll go,' Mac said. 'You keep juggling, and

maybe Belle can start on the phone calls.' He took his list from Izzy and passed it over to Belle, talking to her in a quiet voice, suggesting what she might say, emphasising it was a precautionary move but it was better to be safe than sorry.

As he whisked out of the room, Izzy let out the breath she'd been holding. What *was* it about this man that had her so uptight? So dithered and confused?

Another soft chime and she knew she was needed. The rosters would have to wait, and as for unanswerable questions—well, those she had to put right out of her mind.

What was quite a large room for a country ED was filling up rapidly—filling up with worried-looking mothers or fathers, each clutching a small child by the hand.

'Dr Mac told me to phone the pre-school earlier,' the enrolled nurse on duty told her, 'and they must have started contacting parents straight away.'

Izzy could see Mac in a curtained alcove already, speaking to an anxious father. He saw Izzy, excused himself, and came across to her.

'We'll do antibiotic jabs today and ask parents to check their child's immunisation schedule and come back if they need the vaccine.'

'Sounds good,' Izzy said. 'I'll rustle up a few more nurses or aides to organise this scrum.'

As the day wore on, the trickle of people who'd been in contact with Rhia became a flood. Mac had contacted Braxton for more antibiotic and warned they could also be needing vaccine.

He was, Izzy realised when they had a break in customers late afternoon, the most organised doctor she'd ever worked with, and his efficiency seemed to make the whole process move more smoothly.

Swing shift nurses and aides had come in, taking over from anyone who had to go off duty on time to collect children or meet appointments, but the flood was once again a trickle and all but Izzy had returned to normal duties.

Mac was sitting behind the reception desk, eating a sandwich that had grown stale enough to have the edges of the bread curling up in a most unappetising manner.

'Want some?' he said.

'Eugh! No way! I did grab something earlier but I'm going to make a cuppa while the place is quiet. Do you want one?'

He shook his head, lifting a can of soda that was sitting on the desk.

But the image of him, sandwich in one hand, soda in the other, stayed with Izzy as she hurried to the tea room.

He was just a man, an ordinary man—good doctor, though—but still just a man!

So why was he affecting her the way he was?

Why so instantly?

Why him when other men roused no emotion whatsoever?

It must be, she finally decided, just one of life's mysteries to which there was no answer—no logical explanation.

CHAPTER SEVEN

Mac watched her disappear out the door and wondered about attraction. Why one woman and not another?

He looked at the curling edge of the sandwich and decided she'd been right—it wasn't worth eating. Dumping it and the empty can in the bin, he picked up the ED admissions book, looking back through the pages, seeing more than one night a week when they had no patients at all.

Had he brought the rush of emergencies to this small town?

That was nearly as ridiculous a thought as the attraction one he'd had earlier!

But forcing himself to focus—so as not to think about the other matter—he could see that this time of the day was always quiet. Patients, it seemed, came into the ED late afternoon, three to five, then the numbers dropped off until six-thirty when another trickle might arrive.

With the news about Rhia spreading, tonight's trickle would more likely be a flood.

'Will we have extra staff on this evening in case the people Belle phoned start coming in?' he asked Izzy, who was coming through the door with her cup of tea.

'Yes, we will,' a voice that wasn't Izzy's answered, and he realised Roger was right behind her. 'But I mean "we", not "you". Time the pair of you were off. The hospital can't afford overtime, you know.' He smiled, then added, 'Well, not the amount of overtime you've racked up over the weekend. Izzy doesn't count as she wasn't even on duty so how could she possibly claim overtime?'

As a nurse Mac had met, but whose name he couldn't remember, had followed Roger into the room, it was hard to argue.

'I'm happy to leave you to it,' Mac said, then turned to Izzy. 'And as I've just thrown my lunch into the bin and I know you haven't eaten, how about we duck into town for an early dinner at that Thai restaurant you mentioned? I've a few things to go over with Roger, so you'd have time to slip home and change.'

He hesitated, then added, 'Nikki might like to come, too—save you having to feed her.'

Was it nothing more than a friendly gesture, or was it a test? Izzy wondered. She'd told him she hadn't dated because she didn't want men coming in and out of Nikki's life, so asking Nikki made it just a casual dinner.

Didn't it?

And asking in front of other staff, that was casual, too—or had he done *that* to make it hard for her to refuse?

'Go and change, the man said.' Roger's voice broke into her muddled thoughts. 'No one in their right mind wants to be seen eating in town with someone in that appalling uniform.'

'It's practical and not that appalling!' She automatically defended the uniform Hallie had chosen, although Izzy had never yet met anyone it suited.

'Just go!' Roger ordered, and she went.

Befuddled, that was what she was.

And tired now the let-down after a busy day was seeping into her body.

Better tiredness than the things she felt when she was with Mac.

So why was she going to dinner with him? *Again!*

With him and Nikki—that sounded better, and felt better, too, the tiredness leaving her as she wondered whether the two would get on well.

'Fab!' was Nikki's reaction. 'Shan and I can get on with the project.'

'After you've eaten,' Izzy told her firmly. 'Mac was good enough to ask us both so you'll sit and eat with us. It's an early dinner so if you like Shan could come back here with us and stay over if you've work you'd like to do.'

Nikki surprised her with a warm hug.

'You're the greatest, Mum!'

And Izzy's heartbeats went erratic again, although a very different kind of erratic from the way it reacted to Mac.

Enough! Shower and change, go downtown and eat with the man, then home to bed.

Inviting Nikki to dinner was nothing more than kindness.

As for the attraction—well, that was nothing but chemistry, a reaction.

Like a nuclear explosion?

Ridiculous, but that was how it felt—sudden and totally inexplicable, but so powerful…

She *really* shouldn't be seeing him again tonight!

She left the shower and dressed quickly, pulling on a long shift that swirled about her ankles.

Hair!

Always a problem, but tonight there was no time to fight it so she rammed combs into each side to hold the rebellious curls back off her face. If she hadn't spent so long in the shower, pondering imponderables, she could have put it up, but it was too late for regrets.

She grabbed a shawl to put around her shoulders in case the night turned cool, and walked into the living room, calling to her daughter.

Rather to her surprise, Nikki's clothes were, for her, remarkably conservative—jeans and a blue and white striped top.

'What, no holes or rips in your gear?' Izzy teased, and Nikki laughed.

'I didn't want to embarrass your doctor friend on our first family date.'

'He is not my friend and it's not a date,' Izzy retorted, then plunged into further trouble. 'Well, he is a friend the way colleagues become friends but it definitely isn't a date.'

They were walking down the path to the doctor's house by now, so Izzy couldn't see Nikki's face when her daughter asked, 'Why not a date, Mum? Is it because of me?'

Izzy sighed.

'Not really, although probably, early on, yes, I worried you might get to like a man I was seeing then he'd disappear, then later I worried—'

'About me being affected by you having someone else? Shared love? Possible abuse?'

'You're too smart for your own good,' Izzy

said, putting her arm around Nikki's shoulders and giving her a hug.

'Not really,' Nikki told her. 'You can't help hearing and reading about all that kind of thing, but it's time you had someone special in your life, Mum. I'm old enough and we're close enough for me to tell you if I thought anyone was creepy. I mean, I know Roger's always giving me a pat but he's not creepy, not like that cleaner you had at the hospital a few years back. He was an old man—'

'At least forty,' Izzy put in.

'Old!' Nikki reiterated. 'He used to give Shan and me lollies and then we'd run away.'

Sheesh! Izzy knew exactly who Nikki meant but this was the first she'd heard of the lollies. The man hadn't been there long, mainly because other staff members were uneasy about him, but if she hadn't known *that* about her daughter what else might she not know?

'Mum, we're here, and there's Mac waiting at his gate and I know you're thinking bad mother thoughts but, really, we were fine and if we'd told you, you'd have put a stop to it and we liked the lollies.'

'You okay?' Mac asked, touching Izzy lightly on the shoulder.

Fortunately she was so numbed by what Nikki had just told her that the electricity that flashed through her body was only a half-charge, although her knees felt wobbly and she was pleased when he hooked his arm through hers, his other arm through Nikki's, and led them down towards the town.

'Not often I get to take *two* beautiful women out to dinner,' Mac said.

Then he laughed when Nikki retorted with, 'Flatterer!'

She then asked him about the meningococcal, having heard about it at school.

'I've had the vaccine—actually, I've had every vaccine ever developed, thanks to an over-anxious mother.'

She was teasing Izzy, Mac knew, but there was a gentleness in it that suggested a maturity beyond her age.

Growing up in a house with grandparents, as Hallie and Pop surely were?

Not that he had time to ponder the question, for she was speaking again.

'Sorry, miles away, what did you ask?' he said.

'Do you know anything about global warming?'

'Nikki!' Izzy protested, 'Let's just have a nice peaceful dinner without any debates on the problems of the world.'

'It's for my project, and he's a doctor—he'd know a lot of science.'

Time to intervene, Mac decided, though he'd far rather just keep walking, feeling the warmth of Izzy by his side, imagining how things could be—might be?

Probably wouldn't be…

'But not how to cure global warming, Nikki,' Mac told her. 'It's something that's going to take a lot of research and there still won't be a vaccine for it, but what, apart from sharks and global warming, do you do at school? You're in high school, right?'

Nikki listed off her subjects, gave character sketches—not always good but none too bad—of her teachers, and by that time they'd reached the restaurant and he had to relinquish his hold on Izzy.

Which was just as well, because seeing her in the bright advertising lights outside, his body tightened, his lungs seized, and he rather thought he might be shaking.

This was ridiculous!

Or was it, when she looked so ravishing? Red hair pushed back so it was a mass of rioting curls behind her head. A long dress with swirling patterns of what looked like autumn leaves, skimming across her lithe figure, emphasising pert breasts, a slim waist and hips that were designed to be held, in order to draw her closer.

'Are we going in, or are you going to stand there all night, staring at Mum?'

Had he been staring?

Surely not—he wasn't some schoolboy seeing his first woman.

Besides, the last thing she wanted in her li
right now was a man…

He shuffled the pair of them in front of hi
into the restaurant, although it was an effo
not to feel the silky material of that miraculo
dress.

Miraculous dress?

He was losing it!

Or maybe he'd spent so many years seeir
women in camouflage or uniform or khaki f.
tigues that the dress had affected him.

The dress or the woman inside it?

Nikki was introducing him to Shan's moth
who ran the front of house at the restaurant. Sl
led them to a table in a quiet alcove, leavir
them with menus and a bottle of cold water.

'You've had too big a day,' Izzy said to hir
'You look punch-drunk!'

'You've had a bigger day and you look ma;
nificent!'

'She does, doesn't she?' Nikki said, addin;
with the candour of youth, 'That's Mum's f
vourite dress.'

Izzy blushed and shook her head, then filled her water glass and drank deeply, thankful she didn't have a coughing fit or embarrass herself in some other way, given that her daughter had already mortified her.

Mac's head was bent over the menu, Nikki's close to his as she pointed out the best dishes, and seeing the pair of them Izzy felt a pang of conscience.

Maybe she should have done something about finding a father for Nikki earlier. Back when she was little—starting at pre-school where other kids had fathers—she'd sometimes asked about hers, but as none of them had a clue who'd fathered her sister's baby, Izzy could only tell the truth, that not even her sister had known.

At four, Nikki had accepted it, but Izzy knew that any day now Nikki would begin to wonder about a mother who hadn't known who her baby's father was. She knew her mother had been sick and died, but not about the drugs—something else that would have to be a conversation soon.

Izzy sighed, and Mac turned towards her.

'You don't have a favourite? It's too hard to choose?'

He smiled and her toes curled obligingly and she was glad they were sitting, with her feet tucked safely under the table, so no one could see *that* reaction. Perhaps in future she should wear shoes, not sandals, when out with Mac.

Although there was no real reason why she should be out with Mac again, and plenty of reasons why she shouldn't.

'I'm having the chicken pad Thai and coconut prawns,' Nikki announced, and, too bamboozled by her emotions, Izzy took the easy way out.

'I'll have the same,' she said, then caught Nikki's questioning look.

'You're going to eat noodles in front of Mac? And in your favourite dress?' her daughter said, in a voice that couldn't have been more incredulous. 'You know what a mess you always get into with noodles.'

'Not always,' Izzy said weakly, but with Mac now looking at her she wasn't about to back out.

She got into a mess with the noodles. For reasons beyond her comprehension, where other people could manipulate their spoons and forks to get them neatly into their mouths, the best she could manage was to get one end in and slurp the rest, leaving the juice all down her chin.

Or the whole lot fell out of the spoon as she lifted it towards her chin and she splattered herself, the tablecloth and anyone within arm's length of the disaster.

Nikki refrained from saying 'I told you so', and Mac was super-helpful with extra napkins, but if she'd thought her daughter's mention of her favourite dress was mortifying, this was fifty times worse and probably had a special name but she didn't know it.

The meal was delicious, and Shan's mother insisted it was on the house, but as they left Izzy realised that suggesting Shan return with them to stay the night hadn't been such a good idea. The pair went on ahead, way ahead, and the chatter and laughter drifting back grew fainter and fainter.

'Are they making sure we're left on our own for the walk home?' Mac asked.

'I'm afraid so,' Izzy answered gloomily. 'It seems Nikki's decided I need a man in my life and as long as you don't have a demented ex-lover then you'll do!'

'I'm flattered. And, no, no demented ex-lover.'

Their stroll had slowed so much they were dawdling and as they reached the deep shadows of the old fig tree he paused, touching her lightly on the shoulder to turn her towards him.

'And what about you?' he asked quietly. 'Would I do for you?'

It was too dark to see any reaction on her face but he watched her shake her head.

'It's all too hard just now,' she murmured. 'And you really don't want this either, for all the attraction there is between us.'

'So you do feel it?'

His voice was rough with some emotion he didn't understand, but the kiss he dropped on her lips was nothing more than a breath of air—the brush of a butterfly's wing.

Yet he felt the tremor that ran through her body, felt it in her shoulder where his hand still rested lightly.

He wanted her in a way he'd never felt before, yet knew it couldn't be. She wouldn't—couldn't—take the risk of losing her child, although how realistic that risk was he wasn't sure.

Neither was she a woman he could dally with—she was too fine, too caring, too loving and the way he was, his head still in a mess, nightmares roaring through his sleep—he'd end up hurting her.

Yet he couldn't let her go—couldn't ease her away when she leant into him—couldn't *not* kiss her when she raised her face to his, her lips an unseen invitation in the gloom beneath the tree.

Long and deep, this kiss! He probed her lips, tasted them with his tongue, felt her mouth open to the unspoken invitation and was lost. His arms wrapped around her, clamping her body to his, and his heart beat with a frenzied tattoo against his ribs.

She breathed his name, her fingers on his face now, moving across his cheeks, his temple, learning him through touch while he learnt the secrets of her mouth, the taste of her, her soft shape against his hardness.

It knew no bounds, this kiss, until the need to breathe, to replenish empty lungs with air, forced their heads apart. Knees weak, he stepped back to rest against the massive trunk of the tree, Izzy moving with him, still in his arms.

And with her hands now framing his face, which he knew would be nothing more than a faint oval in the darkness, she whispered, 'Do you really think a short affair would cure this? Do you think it would ever be enough?'

He drew her close again, his lips moving against her hair, kissing as he answered.

'I have no idea,' he said, because honesty was suddenly important. 'I'd be willing to find out, but you're the one with most at stake, my lovely one, so it's up to you.'

He felt her slump, as if her bones had melted, felt her head shake against his chest.

'I don't know!'

The plaintive response cut into him, as painful as a knife wound.

'Then let's just wait until you do,' he told her, straightening up from the tree, steadying her with his hands, brushing his fingers over her hair, then his thumb across her lips.

'We'll wait,' he repeated, then took her hand and led her out of the darkness, seeing the redness of her well-kissed lips, the glow of colour in her cheeks, and the doubt that shadowed the happiness in her eyes.

Back on the footpath, hands unlatched, they walked briskly up past the hospital and onto the path to the old nunnery.

'I'm sorry to be such a wuss about this,' she muttered as they reached the place where she'd disappeared before. 'But I really don't know where I stand and whether the adoption could be threatened and—well, I don't know anything at all right now—my brain's stopped working.'

'It's been a long day,' Mac told her, although

what he really wanted to do was kiss away the hopelessness he knew she was feeling.

'Too long,' she agreed, then straightened up and actually smiled at him.

'Thank heavens I invited Shan back for the night. It means the two of them will be shut away in Nikki's room and I can sneak in without a post mortem of the evening and an inquisition on why it took us so long to get home.'

He smiled and touched her dimple.

'Good luck with that,' he said, and watched as she did the disappearing thing again, although this time he did see the door through which she vanished.

Izzy made her way slowly up to the flat. She knew her hair would be a mess but hoped, in case she did run into Nikki or Shan, she didn't look as well kissed as she felt.

It had been a mistake, kissing Mac, but that oh-so-light touch of his lips on hers had weakened her to such an extent she could do no more than slump against him, and lift her lips...

For more?

Of course for more!

The man was right, this attraction—or chemical reaction—that had sizzled between them from that first meeting on the beach was too strong to be ignored.

Yet ignore it she should.

Unless he was right, and having a quick affair might let it fizzle out...

How quick was a quick affair?

Nikki probably knew more about relationships than she did—from second-hand experience admittedly.

Not that she could discuss this with Nikki...

Or anyone really...

Although—

She ran her mind quickly over the much-loved people she considered sisters and brothers. Lila had absolutely no experience with men, determined to find out who she was before she became someone else as part of a pair. Marty was an expert on affairs and would undoubtedly say, *Go for it, Iz!* because that was how he lived his life.

Stephen, now...

Sir Stephen they'd always called him when they wanted to tease, because of all of them he had family that actually wanted him—two families, in fact—wealthy ones at that—two sets of grandparents fighting for the right to bring him up, in and out of courts, while Steve fitted himself awkwardly into Hallie and Pop's chaotic family.

She had no idea about Steve's love life. Nikki's mother had always been the one closest to Stephen, living with him in Sydney off and on, infuriating him with her behaviour, her addictions, her irresponsibility. Yet he'd always taken her in whenever she'd needed a bed, helped her when she'd needed help.

Perhaps that's why he'd been so good to her, Izzy, when she'd struggled with Nikki as a baby. And remembering that, she knew he'd say don't jeopardise the adoption!

She sighed. Fat lot of help her family were!

She showered, ran a comb through her hair, and climbed into bed, exhausted by the day and the emotions but unable to sleep because the kiss played over and over in her head, remembered ripples and tremors of desire tormenting her body.

CHAPTER EIGHT

MAC FELT AT a loss, arriving at the hospital the next morning to find it an Izzy-free zone. A quick check of the rosters showed she wouldn't be on until two, which was, he decided, probably a good idea.

But a recent idea?

He checked again and, yes, there'd been a shuffle in the rosters.

Was she avoiding him?

Had she spent the night reminding herself of all the reasons why getting involved with him could harm her adoption plans?

His night had been tortured not by nightmares but by thoughts of a single kiss, and by images of where that kiss might lead in the future.

Not that he had reason to be optimistic. He was well aware just how important Nikki was to her, and understood her reluctance to jeopardise the adoption process.

But even if they had to wait—surely what was just paperwork couldn't take too long...

'Are you with us or off with the fairies?'

He looked up from his desk where he'd been staring blankly at Izzy's name on the roster, and assured Abby he was all present and correct.

'Very army,' she said. 'Anyway, there are people stacking up in the ED for antibiotic shots and although Aisha—a local GP, have you met her?—is helping out, it's getting hectic.'

'Yes, I've met Aisha and, yes, I'll come,' he said, pushing himself up from the chair, pushing away memories of a splinter of time beneath the huge old tree, and turning his mind to what lay ahead.

At least he'd checked on Rhia and the Watsons when he'd first arrived, pleased to see the little girl was no worse.

Somehow he and Aisha got through the flood of panicky residents, many of whom, he guessed, hadn't had any contact with the Watsons, and by the time they stopped for a late lunch things had settled down. But Izzy's arrival coincided with the local ambulance, bringing in a ten-year-old boy who'd fallen in the school playground, suspected broken arm.

Izzy heard the ambulance approaching as she walked down to work. No flashing lights and sirens but she knew its noise as well as that of her own car.

Would Mac be in the ED, alerted ahead of the new arrival?

She'd woken in a stupid panic, unsure how to face a man with whom she'd shared such a fiery kiss the night before, and, given how the rosters had been disrupted the previous day, it had been easy to switch her shift time.

But she had to face him sometime—face him in daylight or the bright lights of the hospital—and put the kiss behind her. Behind them both.

The ambulance attendant was bringing a small boy through the doors, a white-faced, frightened small boy clutching at his right arm, which was stabilised in a sling.

Izzy went to him immediately, all thoughts of kisses gone from her head.

'And what have you done to yourself, Kurt Robson?' she teased, kneeling beside him and putting her arm around his shoulder.

'Fell over, that's all, but it hurts.'

'Of course it does.'

She looked up at the ambo.

'Have his parents been contacted?'

'His mum's on the way.'

'That's great, isn't it, Kurt?'

Kurt's face suggested it might not be that great.

'Mum might be angry,' he muttered. 'When I hurt my foot she was. She said I was playing too roughly, but this time, truly, I just fell over.'

'That's okay, we'll sort things out with Mum.'

'We gave him seven mils of paracetamol for the pain but that's all he's had,' the ambo said, handing the paperwork over to Izzy and heading for the door, and probably a late lunch.

Kurt's mother and Mac arrived at the same time, one through the front ED entrance, the other from the hospital.

'He had a fall,' Izzy told Mac, trying desperately to remind her body that this was work and she could handle colleague-to-colleague stuff for all that her blood was singing through her veins at the mere sight of him.

Who knew what a casual touch might do?

Turn her brain to mush, that's what, she realised when he brushed against her as he, too, knelt to talk to the boy.

Okay—enough's enough!

She breathed deeply and moved away to greet Mrs Robson, then Mac was by her side, speaking quietly to her.

'It should just be a simple X-ray; we do that here, don't we?'

Izzy nodded, the deep breath not quite stabilising her yet.

'I can actually do a bit more than that. With my pre-med degree I added a thirteen-week radiography course—before Nikki. We don't have an MRI machine but we can most other radiography.'

'Wonder Woman!' Mac teased softly, undoing the small amount of good that deep breathing had effected.

'Not really,' Izzy responded, letting a little of the irritation she was feeling because of him seep into her voice. 'You're probably just as capable of most radiography stuff as I am. Every doctor can do a simple X-ray.'

He grinned at her but she refused to be charmed.

Colleagues, they were colleagues! She'd work out the rest later.

Much later…

But thoughts of charm and singing blood disappeared when Izzy shoved the X-ray film into the light box. The same picture would be on the screen at the ED's front desk and she knew Mac was looking at it there.

'Mac!'

He came immediately and she wondered if he'd seen what she'd seen and realised it wasn't something to discuss in front of the Robsons.

'What are you seeing?' he asked, and she

pointed to the fine line that showed a break in the humerus.

'That's the obvious one, but look at the elbow joint—isn't it slightly distorted?'

Mac ran his finger over the picture then turned his attention to the shoulder joint.

'That seems loose as well. Has the boy had other fractures, do you know?'

'None that have been reported here, but he said Mum got angry when he hurt his foot.'

'Okay, let's get him back in here and look at the foot,' Mac said, leaving with a touch on her shoulder that was so light she might have imagined it.

She heard him talking to Mrs Robson and Kurt, explaining they wanted to do some more checking.

'Is there anyone in your family that's had broken bones before?' he was asking Mrs Robson.

'Well, most kids do, don't they?' she said. 'I know I had a broken leg when I was younger.'

'And you went mad at me when I hurt my foot!' Kurt put in, and his mother laughed.

'Mothers worry,' she said, patting down his unruly brown hair.

Mac lifted Kurt onto the X-ray table while Izzy focused the camera over the foot he'd hurt earlier. Mac escorted Mrs Robson from the room while Izzy checked she'd get what she wanted.

'Hold still again,' she said, slipping into the side room and pressing the button to activate the camera.

She took different angle shots, propping the little foot with foam pads, and when she was satisfied she returned him to his mother, who by this time was getting anxious, although someone had given her a cup of tea and plate of biscuits.

This time they studied the shots on the computer in the radiography office, enlarging details so they could easily see the two metatarsals that had thickened areas where breaks had healed.

'Brittle bones?' Izzy asked. 'I've heard of it but wasn't sure it existed as a condition.'

'OI,' Mac replied. 'Osteogenesis imperfecta—there are eight levels of it, with the first four being the most common. OI One is the best to have, and probably what young Kurt has, and often people can go through all their lives without knowing they have it.'

'Genetic?' Izzy asked, so absorbed in learning something new that the fact that she was shoulder to shoulder with Mac wasn't bothering her at all.

'Usually, but not always. The problem is, we could set his arm but with OI I'm not sure that it shouldn't be pinned. I think someone said the other day that there's an orthopaedic specialist in Braxton.'

'Paul Kent,' Izzy told him. 'Very good. Should we get the ambulance back to take them?'

Mac had straightened and now turned towards her, a slight smile greeting her question.

'I think that's best, don't you? Although it leaves Mrs Robson stuck there without a vehicle.'

Colleagues, Izzy reminded herself, ignoring the effect of that slightest of smiles.

'If Paul decides to operate, Mrs Robson will want to stay anyway, and her husband has a ute so he can take over anything they need when he finishes work.'

Mac nodded and left the room, leaving Izzy to turn off machines and tidy up.

He was on the phone to the specialist when she returned to the ED and the ambulance was pulling in.

'Can I phone someone to pick up your car?' she asked Mrs Robson, who shook her head.

'I've called my sister—she only lives down the road, she'll walk up and get it. She has the extra set of keys to it and the house so she can pack things for me and Kurt—better than my husband would.'

She smiled and Izzy realised that however Mac had explained the situation it had left the woman at ease, not anxious and distracted as many mothers would be.

'Osteogenesis imperfecta—I like learning new things,' she said to Mac as the ambulance departed. 'I know we covered something about brittle bones in the course I did but I'm sure I didn't hear that name.'

'It's not that common,' Mac told her, 'but learning new things—well, that happens all the time.'

She knew he was teasing—suggesting—but also knew she had to ignore it. That kiss last night—and where it might lead—was something she had to think seriously about.

'Then I'd better go and learn new things about what's been happening at the hospital all day. I haven't even signed on for my shift, let alone had any kind of handover.'

'Of course,' he said, and something in his voice told her he understood she was backing off, trying to ignore what had happened between them.

Mac headed for his office, only too aware that there was paperwork multiplying on his desk, pleased to have a really boring distraction.

Seeing Izzy—a far from boring distraction—had reminded him that a relationship with a colleague was not a good idea. In fact, it was a dreadful idea! Especially when he was new to the job of being a civilian doctor, and really needed to concentrate on doing that job well.

Belle came in with a message for him. Paul

Kent had received the X-rays and would phone him after he'd seen Kurt.

He thought of Izzy repeating the diagnosis, her face alight with learning something new, and his gut knotted.

The thought of *not* having a relationship with that particular colleague was far too depressing to even contemplate. Somehow they had to make this work—not only the being colleagues part of it but the hesitation they both felt about involvement.

Very reasonable hesitation!

'Are you sighing over the paperwork?' Belle asked, bringing in a sheaf of more bumf. 'One thing I can tell you, if you don't get onto it, it just multiplies. Worse than rabbits, paperwork.'

He laughed but knew what she said was true, so he set aside all thoughts of the redhead beetling around somewhere in the building and concentrated on sorting the urgent from the non-urgent, the notices of new procedural policy from the important things that needed a response.

Izzy started her catching up with a visit to Rhia. As Mac had said, she was holding her own, although she was still pale and from the chart slightly feverish. Ben was in the room with her.

'I've sent Sally home to get some sleep.'

He twisted his hands together as he spoke then looked up at Izzy.

'She *will* get better, won't she?' he asked, and the desperation in his voice touched Izzy's heart.

'We'll do everything we can to make sure she does,' she promised. 'She's getting the best of care, the drugs we're giving her will be fighting the infection, and...'

She hesitated, mainly because she hated making promises she couldn't keep.

'They usually win,' she finished, hoping he had missed the pause. 'It just takes time,' she told him, 'so you and Sally have to look after yourselves because even after she's out of here, she could need a long convalescence.'

'We'll make sure we're there for her,' Ben promised. Then his head lifted again and his dark eyes met Izzy's. 'I know all parents think their kids are special, but she's especially precious to us. Sally had a couple of miscarriages before Rhia and hasn't been able to get pregnant since. We've thought about IVF because we'd love another child, but we'd have to go to the city, and it's so expensive.'

'It's becoming more affordable, so who knows,' Izzy told him, not mentioning that her brother Steve was already talking about setting up a private IVF clinic right here in Wetherby.

She smiled as she thought about his grandiose plan of building a relaxing seaside resort where couples could stay while they underwent fertility treatment or IVF programmes. He believed that the failures in IVF conception were often brought on by stress and his clinic resort could alleviate a lot of that.

So Steve was in her mind when she ran into Mac in the tea room.

'Shouldn't you be at home, cooking up a Moroccan delicacy? Your shift's long finished.'

'Paperwork,' he said succinctly, turning from

the urn where he was making a coffee to offer to make one for her.

'No, tea for me at this time of the evening,' she said. 'I don't need any stimulants to keep me from sleep tonight.'

He found a teabag and made her a tea, raising a milk bottle in silent query.

She shook her head and he passed her the rather battered mug.

Inevitably their fingers touched, and he raised his eyebrows as he asked, 'Something keep you from sleep last night? Stimulation?'

Izzy gave a huff of laughter.

'Not that so much as where it could lead,' she told him as one of the enrolled nurses came looking for Izzy.

'It's Mrs Warren in bed nine,' she said. 'Says she's feeling right poorly, whatever that might mean.'

'I'll see to her,' Izzy said quietly, setting her tea down on the table and leaving the room. Mrs Warren should really be in a hospice, but the nearest one was in Braxton and she didn't want to leave her friends and family.

She *was* poorly, her skin sagging around her bones, her old eyes clouded with pain and confusion. Three months earlier she'd been an extremely fit and spritely ninety-three-year-old living by herself, capable of managing her house and garden, getting a little help with shopping and occasional visits from a social worker.

An accident in the bathroom, a fall that had left her with a broken hip, bruised ribs and a bang on the head had changed all that. Lying in bed, she was a prime victim for pneumonia, and although she seemed to have fought that off, she was still far from well, her organs slowly closing down.

Izzy slipped into the chair beside her and took her hand, talking quietly to her.

'I see someone's brought you flowers from your garden,' she said, nodding towards the big bunch of colour on a shelf on the wall.

'Jimmy,' Mrs Warren whispered. 'He's a good lad. He comes every day and often brings a mate so we can have a laugh, but I don't want to laugh any more, Izzy. I've had enough.'

'I know, love,' Izzy soothed. 'I know.'

Mrs Warren's health directory had been explicit that she didn't want measures taken to keep her alive, but her heart refused to give in, still beating strongly in the old woman's skeletal body.

Izzy sat with her until she drifted off to sleep, then she checked the other patients under her care. With everything quiet she returned to Mrs Warren, sitting with her through the night until, at four, her heart finally gave in, and the old woman passed away.

Technically, one of the GPs was on call for the night shift, but why wake him just to certify death when Mac would be here at six? Possibly earlier, knowing Mac. Declaring Mrs Warren dead could wait, as could breaking the news to her family.

Izzy had wanted to call them earlier, but Mrs Warren had insisted she didn't want wailing relatives sitting around her bed.

'I'm happy to go,' she'd told Izzy, 'so there's no reason for tears.'

She was phoning Mrs Warren's eldest daughter when Mac arrived.

'What are you doing here?' he demanded. 'Have you done a double shift?'

Izzy held up a hand to silence him as someone answered the phone and she began her explanation.

Mac shook his head and left the nurses' station, but when he returned it wasn't to chide her. Instead, he touched her lightly on the arm.

'You sat with her all night?'

Izzy nodded.

'She didn't want the family, just someone to be there.'

'You should have had the coffee,' Mac said, but the glint in his eyes and the smile tugging at his lips told her he approved.

Probably would have done the same, Izzy realised, and the warmth his light touch had generated blossomed into appreciation.

He was a good man.

It was a refrain that stayed with her as her feet pounded on the coastal path. She'd had to run to clear her head and have any hope of sleep but the 'good man' thought stuck and she knew it tipped the scales in his favour in the matter of any relationship between them.

Mac got on with his working day with a certain sense of relief. Relief because he'd see much less of Izzy while she was on the swing shift from two till ten, but qualifying the relief was a touch of let-down.

Damn it all, he *liked* seeing her at work! Enjoyed a glimpse of her red curls as she flashed past a door, enjoyed the feel of her by his side as they studied notes or discussed a patient.

The worst of it was he'd see even less of her out of working hours. It was unlikely she'd want to try his Moroccan tagine at ten-thirty at night.

He fought an urge to check the nursing rosters again—he'd checked twice already today and she was definitely on the swing shift. And today he wouldn't see her come on duty. He had a district hospital meeting—some kind of meet and greet the new guy, he guessed—at Braxton Hospital at two this afternoon.

Belle had booked him into a motel in Braxton for the night as apparently there was always an informal dinner held after these meetings.

The paperwork following Mrs Warren's death diverted him for a few minutes and a visit to the nursing home took up a little more time, but the day still loomed as a very long one without Izzy.

Until a very attractive blonde bounced into his office.

'I'm Frances, I'm your physiotherapist—well, not yours particularly but the hospital one. I do two days a week in Wetherby, one here at the hospital and tomorrow in a private practice. I'm based in Braxton, so some of the patients here I've already seen at the hospital there.'

'Like the young man whose ankle was pinned and plated in Braxton last weekend? I heard he was coming back to us today.'

'And you've got another man from the same

accident—simple tib and fib break who'll be seeing me here as an outpatient.'

Mac nodded. He'd discharged the patient with the simple break after fitting a full cast and had talked to him about needing physio once the cast came off, but apparently Frances would have exercises he could do now.

He walked with her as she visited the occupied rooms, introducing the Watsons and little Rhia, pleased that Frances spoke mostly to Rhia, telling her she'd be back to give her some toys that would help her stay strong in hospital.

'You probably haven't explored the physio cupboard,' Frances said as they left the room.

'I've seen a room that looked to be full of toys, and I did wonder just how many children might ever be here at any one time to warrant so many.'

Leaving Frances to go about her work, Mac returned to his office, aware of how much he didn't know about the hospital he was supposedly running. What other visiting therapists might they have? How did he contact one if he needed someone for a specific patient? An OT for a stroke patient, for instance?

All the information he needed would be here in his office somewhere, but he'd avoided being in it, doing only the absolutely necessary paper-work—and then only when bullied into it by Belle.

True, there had been emergencies to be dealt with in his first few days, and Rhia's diagnosis had led to a flood of outpatients, but now things had quietened down, it was time to learn his job—his real job—especially as the other district doctors would expect him to know *something* at this afternoon's meeting.

'Let's start at the beginning,' he said to Belle when he'd summoned her to his office. 'Tell me everything I need to know about how the place runs. I know who's in charge of Housekeeping, and I have met the cooks, but apart from Frances what other visiting professionals do we have? Where do I find their information?'

He smiled at her.

'I fear I've been leaving everything to you.'

'Not your fault,' Belle assured him. 'You've hardly had a moment to breathe since you arrived.'

But she ran him through the normal weekly and monthly routines, through the visiting professionals, and volunteers who worked mainly in the nursing home, playing board games and doing craft projects with the residents.

'It's all in there somewhere,' she said, waving her hand at the filing cabinets banked against one wall, 'but generally you only need to ask me and I'll either find it for you or find out what you want to know.'

'In fact, you really run the place,' Mac said, smiling at her. 'I had a sergeant like that in the army.'

They talked a little longer, Mac realising just how much was involved in running even a small hospital.

Frances appeared at the door, greeted Belle like an old friend, then handed Mac a knobby ball.

'Stress ball,' she said. 'You just squeeze it in your hand—one hand at a time—you'll be surprised how much it will relieve that tension in your neck and shoulders.'

What tension in my neck and shoulders? Mac wanted to ask, but with Belle there...

And Frances was right, although how she'd noticed it he didn't know.

'Thanks,' he said, taking the ball and squeezing it in his right hand then throwing it across the table to Belle, wanting to make light of it— to not have people thinking he couldn't cope.

'Want a go?' he said, but Belle only tossed it back.

'I've got one of my own,' she said, 'only mine's hot pink. Frances keeps an eye on all of us.'

Enough of an eye to see tension in his neck?

Tension that was part of his PTSD, or new tension caused by his attraction to a certain redhead?

He wondered if the visiting professionals included a psychologist...

Mac kept squeezing, one hand and then the

other, while Belle and Frances were now discussing a barn dance to be held that weekend at a property out of town.

'It's to raise money for the animal shelter,' Frances explained. 'Do come, I'll email you the directions. They have a kind of auction and you can bid on the different animals and if you win the bid your money goes towards its keep for the year.'

He agreed it sounded fun and was about to ask if he could take Izzy along when he realised that being linked with him was probably the last thing she wanted.

Or needed…

'It's very casual,' Frances was explaining, while he squeezed hard on his stress ball.

Because he was thinking of Izzy?

'It really *is* in a barn out on the animal refuge,' Belle added.

'As long as I don't have to wear a hat with corks dangling off it,' Mac told them, and the laughter broke up the meeting.

So, off to Braxton! *And it will probably do you good not to see Izzy for a whole day*, he thought. *That* situation was getting way out of control…

CHAPTER NINE

'WHY ARE YOU doing the swing shift?' Nikki demanded the next morning while Izzy was packing her lunch for school. 'You never do it because it's a quiet one, and working at the weekend means you won't be able to take me to the barn dance.'

'Hallie and Pop will take you,' Izzy said firmly, not answering the real question because she didn't want to admit she'd changed shifts to avoid Mac.

'There's no need because I'm going with Shan and her older brothers and sister,' Nikki informed her, but Izzy barely listened, her mind back to trying to work out why one kiss had affected her so badly.

Badly enough to change shifts in an effort to

avoid the man causing her mind and body so much trouble!

Not that she could avoid him for ever. But she'd hoped the break would give her time to work out what was happening—to rationalise the feelings in her body and remind herself that her first priority was getting through the three- to six-month process of officially adopting her daughter.

Not that it was working—the shift change. She missed seeing Nikki after school, although now she had mornings to catch up with her and hear the latest school news, and she could make sure Nikki was taking a nutritious lunch, but Mac's absence from her life wasn't helping her sort out her thoughts or her feelings.

Even thinking about the kiss sent tremors down her spine, and she couldn't think about the situation without thinking about the kiss so, in truth, she was in a muddle.

A muddle made worse when she saw him as she came on duty that afternoon!

'You avoiding me?' he asked, just enough edge in his voice to tell her it wasn't really a joke.

'Trying to,' Izzy answered honestly, if weakly, as her brain lit up like a fireworks display and her body was rattled by more reactions than it could handle.

'Working, is it?' he asked, so genially she wanted to hit him. How could he be so composed?

Because he was a man?

Because he was used to kissing women he barely knew?

'How was the meeting?' Izzy managed to ask, determined to get her mind focused on work. She'd leave her body till later and run it to exhaustion...

'Very educational.'

Izzy raised her eyebrows, sure he was being facetious.

'No, I mean it,' he assured her, with a smile she really, really didn't need. 'I had no idea of the complexities of coordinating health services in regional areas. Whoever set this all up was a genius. The army couldn't have done it better.'

'High praise indeed,' Izzy said drily.

'No, I mean it. The way they manage to coordinate the staffing of the emergency services, like the ambulance and helicopter, with staffing at the hospitals so there's always a paramedic available to go out to accidents—that alone must take endless fiddling and adjustments.'

'It's a lot of paperwork,' Izzy agreed, and won another unnecessary smile.

'Which most doctors and, I imagine, nurses hate. Yet it all gets done.'

'Because the office staff know the system and have their own procedures in place,' Izzy told him. 'It took quite a while, but at the moment it's working. Most of the time!'

'I'm still mightily impressed,' Mac said.

'Good, but I've got to get to work. Rhia's drip will need changing and apparently the chap who had his ankle fixed in Braxton is complaining about cramps.'

She turned away but not quickly enough to miss Mac's last words, quietly spoken but sneaking into her ears and, damn it, into her heart.

'I've missed you, Izzy!'

The shift was quiet, a few visitors to the ED that Izzy could handle on her own—a footballer with a strained wrist, X-rayed to make sure it wasn't broken, and just before she went off duty, an older man with chest pain but no history of heart problems or angina.

Roger was on call, but by the time he arrived Izzy had ascertained that the ECG was normal, blood pressure and oxygen sat both good, but a blood test showed high troponin levels.

'That's ringing a bell for me,' Roger said. 'We'll admit him anyway and do half-hourly obs but I'll check back through his file.'

Izzy started the process of admitting the man, chatting to him in between the questions she needed to ask.

Yes, he'd been before, feeling the same way, and had stayed three days while the doctors did tests. He'd been to a cardiologist in Braxton who had done more tests, but found nothing.

'And how are you feeling now?' Izzy asked,

as a wardsman arrived to move the patient to a hospital bed.

'The pain's gone but I just don't feel well,' the man explained. 'Just not right.'

Scary, was Izzy's first thought. With no symptoms to treat apart from giving him the blood thinners, there was little they could do but wait and see.

Roger returned as she was accompanying the trolley to a patient room.

'I've found the records of past blood tests. Turns out his blood tests always show a higher level of troponin than is normal. He's had every test under the sun, but the cardiologist found nothing.'

'But we keep him here?'

'My word we do,' Roger said. 'And keep him hooked up to the monitors so we can see if there's the slightest change in his status. High troponin levels could be an indicator of an imminent heart attack, but there've been no studies done on abnormally high levels in an otherwise well person.'

Izzy settled the man into what they considered their 'cardiac ward', a room with monitors already set up so it was only a matter of attaching the leads to their new patient's legs, chest and arms, slipping a blood oxygen monitor onto one finger, and watching information come up on the monitor screen.

'You should be gone,' the night shift nurse told her. 'I've called in an extra nurse so we can keep an eye on him, and Roger's staying awhile, just to be sure.'

Izzy glanced at her watch and realised it was after eleven. Tiredness swamped her suddenly. Adrenalin seeping out, she knew that, but it wasn't helping her put one foot in front of the other as she collected a jacket and headed out the back door for the short walk home.

'Izzy!'

She muffled the shriek that the soft murmur of his voice had caused and turned to see Mac standing in the light shed from the hospital's kitchen window.

'I thought I'd walk you home.'

The moment the words were out of his mouth Mac knew it was probably the lamest thing he'd ever said, but he'd been lurking around the back of the hospital for over an hour, wondering if this constituted stalking, feeling incredibly stupid but needing to see the woman who had him tied in knots.

'May I walk you home?'

She was standing on the path, apparently bemused by his sudden appearance, but then she smiled and he forgot his doubts about stalking, and all but forgot his name.

'That would be nice,' she said, 'although it's quite stupid for you to be doing this. You've got an early shift tomorrow and I imagine the district meeting went on to a dinner and a few drinks last night and you didn't get to bed till all hours.'

But she hadn't said no, so he took her arm and drew her close, felt her warmth, while the effect her body had on his sent blood racing under his skin.

They reached the shadows of the old nunnery

and stopped of one accord, turning to each other as if there was nothing else to do, kissing gently at first, touches of lips on lips, remembering, revelling in their own restraint.

But restraint couldn't hold back the attraction, and the kiss deepened, until Mac heard a low groan from Izzy and she pressed closer, slid her arms around his back, pulling him into her, or her into him, the kiss saying things for which there were no words.

'I want you, Iz,' he murmured when they paused for breath. 'My body aches for you, and I'm sure you feel the same. I know you've got real reservations—that you could be risking the adoption—but surely we could work that out if something happened.'

She stopped his words with kisses, but he pulled away again, smitten by a wild idea.

'We could even get married if things were dicey,' he said, 'and you'd have that family you thought you might get with that other doctor. Mother, father, daughter—a family.'

Izzy sighed but this time didn't kiss him, leaning her head against his chest instead.

'You don't want to get married,' she reminded him.

'Only because the Macphersons, or my branch of them, seem to be genetically challenged when it comes to marriage. My parents have both had plenty of practice at it—the getting married part—but don't seem able to make it stick, and I was obviously a hopeless husband, but if it made things right for you and Nikki we could do it. It wouldn't have to last for ever.'

'Go home,' Izzy told him, stepping backwards so she couldn't touch him again—kiss him again—weaken...

She didn't add that they were just the words every woman wanted to hear—the 'wouldn't have to last for ever' ones.

As if!

She opened the door and slipped inside, without another word to the man she'd been kissing. No way could she tell him that beyond her dream for Nikki had always been another, buried deep because for so long it had seemed impossible—a dream of love and happiness and a marriage that *would* last for ever...

Aware he'd said something wrong, Mac took himself home. Unfortunately, his disappointment at the abrupt end to the kisses wasn't enough to cool his blood or release him from the tension the kisses had caused.

Izzy's body seemed to have imprinted itself on his, so he could feel her pressed against his chest, a ghost lover...

Perhaps the nightmare was inevitable, the roar of planes, the thud of bombs landing, the explosive roar of the devastation that followed.

And he'd mentioned *marriage*?

Expected some woman to put up with the movies that mangled his head at midnight?

His shrink had suggested a relationship might help, hence the dallying, which did seem to stop them.

But would it work for ever?

Could he take the chance?

And why was he even considering it, given how hurriedly Izzy had shied away from the suggestion?

Unable to sleep, he found solace in a book, an easy-to-read mystery he'd found in the house's bookshelves when he'd moved in, so when sleep did come, his thoughts were turning over clues, seeking an answer to the mystery, not thinking of the past, or of a red-headed woman with skin like silk and kisses like magic.

No sign of Mac when Izzy went to work the next afternoon, but it was Saturday, he was off duty although probably on call.

She hoped she didn't need him!

She went about her work, calmly and efficiently, spending some time with Rhia while her parents went out for a walk. The little girl had recovered so quickly Izzy was surprised Mac hadn't discharged her so she could spend the weekend at home, but maybe he feared a relapse.

The young man with the pins and plates in his ankle was complaining about pain, but after checking he'd had pain relief only an hour ear-lier, she decided it was probably boredom and found one of the 'toys' in the physio cupboard that would test his skill—tipping a board to get little balls to run into holes.

It was totally frustrating and she'd only ever seen one patient do it successfully, but she knew that because it *looked* easy most patients, young men in particular, refused to be beaten by it, so it would occupy him for a few hours.

And help him forget his pain…

She caught up with paperwork, told Shan and Nikki they both looked fabulous when they popped in to show off their barn dance outfits—battered jeans, hardly unusual these days, and checked shirts, while the tattered straw hats over cute pigtails completed the look.

'Behave yourself,' she said as Nikki kissed her goodbye, not really worried that her daughter would get up to mischief. All that lay ahead!

But as she handed over to the night shift and prepared to leave work, she was looking forward to getting home and a good night's sleep—undisturbed by memories of kisses from a—

Non-for-ever-and-ever man?

Was that what she could call him?

Definitely a non-marrying type.

He'd spelt that out.

So walking out the back door and hearing the whispered 'Izzy' sent her blood pressure soaring.

'What *are* you doing here?' she demanded. 'You're supposed to be at the dance. They're taking bets at the nursing home on you and Frances getting together.'

'They're what?'

Mac sounded so horrified, Izzy had to laugh.

'They're easily bored,' she said. 'But you should be at the dance. It's expected of the local doctor.'

'I went but you weren't there.'

The words tingled down Izzy's spine.

You can't let him affect you, she told herself, but her body was beyond listening, especially to anything that might be common sense.

'I did leave some money with Belle to buy an animal. I rather fancied the three-legged goat.'

'That's Arthur,' Izzy responded, hoping some normal chit-chat might settle her nerves. 'I kept him a couple of years ago.'

'Lucky Arthur,' Mac murmured, and Izzy knew no amount of chit-chat would work. Her shoulder was already leaning towards his and when he took her hand, her fingers gripped his, joining, intertwining—together...

They walked up the hill, their immediate future as inevitable as it was unspoken. He'd seen her family at the dance, would know—because Nikki was a loudmouth—that the flat would be empty, and suddenly she didn't want to fight this any more. She wanted him in a way she'd never felt before—never even imagined she *could* want someone.

And at this moment for ever was a foreign land, it was the now, and what lay ahead, the now she wanted—needed.

'It's this way,' she said, her voice shaking as,

fingers still linked, she led him through the door...

And into her bedroom...

The hospital grounds were well lit so some light came through the windows, enough for Izzy to see Mac's face as he sought her lips.

She raised her hands and ran them through his hair, holding his head to hers—wanting, needing the kiss to last.

His hands explored her body, her back, her breasts, passing softly over her as if to imprint her on his memory. But as the kiss deepened, the touches, hers and his, became more urgent, more demanding, her fingers tugging at his shirt so she could feel his skin, his easing open the buttons on her uniform to hold one breast in his palm.

A brush of thumb across the nipple and she could feel it peak, moaned softly, then slid her hand between them to find his hardness.

Restraint fled, and hands tore at clothes until they stood naked, close, not touching anywhere but with their lips. Kissing, breathing heavily, his hand between her legs now, hers holding his length in her hand.

'Bed?'

One whispered word, yet she knew he was asking, not suggesting—asking her if it was really what she wanted.

It was to be her decision!

'Bed!' she confirmed, and they fell together, finding each other's bodies close, touching, kissing, prolonging the anticipation, increasing the level of desire to near explosion point.

Mac held her close, felt the moisture in the softness between her legs, heard the gasp of breath, the whisper of need—and knew this wasn't dalliance, though dalliances in the past had left him prepared.

A brief pause, long enough to ensure safe sex but also to wonder why it *wasn't* dalliance, why it felt different. But the moment passed, Izzy's body arching up to his, her pleas for more, for proper contact, inflaming his desire.

Too quickly over, lying together, panting

slightly, drained but content to simply lie, touching, breathing.

No words, but stirrings, too soon surely, but slowly now, with teasing fingers and gentle touches, they drew more pleasure from each other, until Izzy's cry of release was echoed by his own groan of enjoyment, a confirmation of some kind, but of what, he didn't know.

Relaxed together, their talk was general—lovers' talk, of pleasure given and received, widening to talk of their lives, so different, hers made great by the love of strangers, his not really settled until he'd found a home in the army.

How had Wetherby come up?

Later he would ask himself that question a hundred times, but it had, and they talked of the town, the locals, the incomers seeking respite from city life, the refugees rebuilding lives shattered by oppression and war.

So for her to ask, 'How did you come to choose the town?' was almost inevitable, and for him to answer—no problem at all.

She was lying on her side, pressed against

his chest, held in the half-circle of his arm, her golden skin asking for the occasional kiss, a light brush of fingers—eyelids, nose, ears.

'Long ago, so far back it seems like another life,' he told her as he touched, 'I'd just finished my degree, felt freed at last from books and studies and responsibilities. I had leave before I went back to the army, and, like a couple of million other young Aussies do every year, I went to Bali. Have you been?'

He felt her head shake a no against his chest.

'I've heard it's beautiful.'

'It is, a kind of magical place where the real world no longer exists—it's all about the now, and fun, and laughter—beautiful beaches, great surf, nightclubs, and dancing, and gentle people smiling at your antics. It was so relaxing, as I said, another world, with everyone living for not even the day but for the moment.'

Izzy had snuggled closer, and even when he continued, 'I met a girl,' she seemed unbothered.

In fact, she laughed and teased, 'Of course.'

'We spent our time together—two short weeks,

two Aussies having fun—until we walked into the hotel one day and one of the receptionists called out to me. "You're Nicholas Macpherson?" she said, and when I agreed she told me that my father had been hospitalised with a major heart attack and the family wanted me back home.'

He was remembering that time—that moment—so didn't realise Izzy had pulled away, until in the dim light he saw she was sitting on the bed.

'*What* did you say your name was?' she demanded.

Mac stared at her, puzzled by the abrupt change in the mood and by something in her voice.

Should he make light of it?

'Hey, you know me. I'm Mac—we've just made love. Twice.'

'I meant your other name, your whole name?'

This wasn't light—not at all.

Mac sat up, reaching out for her, wanting to hold her, to see her face, but she scrambled off the bed.

'Izzy, what's up?' he asked, totally bamboozled.

'Just tell me your name, your whole name!'

He heard an edge of hysteria in the words, and responded to it.

'Nicholas Edward Macpherson.'

If he'd thought this might calm her down he was totally wrong. Instead, she scrambled around the room, picking up items of clothing and pulling them on, whispering, 'I've got to go, I've got to go. I've got to get out of here, I've got to think.'

He stood up, found his own shorts and pulled them on, then walked tentatively towards her, touching her shoulder to calm her down.

'Iz,' he said gently, 'you live here. It's your place, not mine. But let me help you, tell me what the problem is. Surely there's nothing we can't talk about.'

She turned away from him, shoulders slumped, pressed her head against the window pane and whispered, 'Just go, please, just go!'

He went, although he worried about leaving her alone.

Should he call someone?

Hallie?

And tell her he'd just made passionate love to her daughter but now she seemed to have cracked?

Hardly.

And if there was one word that described Izzy it was sensible. She wouldn't do anything silly.

Would she?

He walked down to his house, poured a whisky, and sat down with it to think.

But where to start?

It was his name that had upset her, but she'd always known his name.

The Macpherson part anyway.

He went back over the conversation and, yes, it was definitely his name that had upset her, but why…

No amount of thinking answered that one so he sent a text, saying he was there for her and please to contact him, any time, because he really needed to know she was okay.

No point in telling her he loved her, although

somewhere along the way, maybe halfway through the whisky, it had occurred to him that that was what he felt for her.

Love!

Could it really be?

It felt like love…

A whole new kind of love…

CHAPTER TEN

NIKKI MAC... NIKKI MAC... The words pounded in Izzy's head as she ran the coast path.

Stupid really when only yesterday—*was* it yesterday?—the refrain had been, 'He's a good man...'

But maybe she was wrong, maybe she should have asked him when he was in Bali, although the sums all added up in her head. She knew his age, and could work back to when he'd got his degree and, anyway, she knew she wasn't wrong.

Nikki Mac. Her sister had texted almost daily about the glory of this Nikki Mac—and of the holiday romance that had no future, although why, she'd never said. She'd been well when she'd gone, had been through a detox programme in Sydney, then given herself the holiday as a reward.

And she'd come back clean, they'd known that, and had stayed clean for months, or so they'd thought because she'd returned straight to Sydney, at first staying with Stephen, then finding a flat and working for a web designer, her dream job.

Until the sleaze bag, as Stephen called her on-again off-again boyfriend, had come back into the picture, tempting their fragile sister with promises of fame—singing in a night club where drugs were plentiful...

Izzy sighed, remembering the lost soul they'd all loved so much. As well as drugs, there'd been a brush with anorexia, and episodes of cutting, so no one had been surprised that Liane, their lovely Liane, hadn't realised she was pregnant.

And hooked again on drugs!

Hallie had flown to Sydney, Stephen had tried to step in, and everyone had forgotten Nikki Mac until the baby came, and with her a grubby piece of paper on which she'd asked Izzy to look after her baby, Nikki.

Izzy's even stride faltered and she brushed tears from her eyes.

Now she knew, it was so obvious—Nikki's blue eyes, the same dark, clear blue...

She shook away the useless thoughts and ran on. She had to think, to work out what to do.

Did she tell?

She *had* to tell?

But who first?

Nikki?

Izzy's usual easy stride faltered again.

What if Nikki chose her father...?

What if Mac *wanted* her?

Mac didn't *do* for ever...

What if Mac *didn't* want her?

Wouldn't that be worse for Nikki?

Worse than not knowing?

Squelching down the howl of agony the thought of losing Nikki caused, Izzy pounded on.

She wouldn't think about it now!

She'd think about it tomorrow...

And having decided that, she turned and headed back towards town, forcing herself to blank out the turmoil in her head, looking at the ocean, drinking in the beauty of her surroundings, smelling the salt in the air, the faint scent of eucalyptus from the scrub, thinking nothing, nothing, nothing...

She heard the ambulance before she saw it, and as she came over the last headland, realised it was heading down to the beach.

A crowd of surfers, boards slung across the sand in a far too haphazard way—Nikki and Shan's project—sharks!

Her feet flew towards the now stationary ambulance, although she knew they'd do everything she'd be able to. She pushed through the gathering crowd, saw the anonymous figure in a full black wetsuit, one leg showing torn, lacerated fabric, skin, blood—

'It's Ahmed,' someone told her. 'Luckily the jet ski had been taking surfers out to the big point break and the rider saw it happen and headed straight over, frightening off the shark and bringing Ahmed in to the beach.'

As she left the beach, Izzy took out her phone

to call his family, then saw Hamid heading down from the esplanade—someone else had already called.

So she went to the hospital instead, showered and pulled on some scrubs, coming out of the staffroom as Mac was asking the ambos to take the trolley through to the resus room.

'Shark bite,' he said to Izzy, as if this was just another day, another crisis, fully expecting her to be there to lend a hand. 'Could you cut off his wetsuit? The pressure of it could be worsening the blood loss. Start with the arms so we can get a drip in. Abby, you set up a cannula as soon as you can.'

They worked in silence except when Mac requested help, stripped the fit young man then laid warmed blankets over his body to help fend off shock. Mac handed tweezers to Izzy.

'Just pick out any neoprene you can see, or anything else that shouldn't be there. Abby, can you flush the wound as Izzy works, flush it hard. I want to X-ray the foot to make sure there are no broken bones, because if there aren't I think we can put him back together again without sending him to Braxton.'

Izzy picked at bits of black material from the tattered skin and flesh and wondered at Mac's confidence.

But he'd no doubt seen worse, the results of bombs or IEDs and had learned to put body parts back together again.

So if anyone could save Ahmed's foot, Mac could.

The X-ray showed no bone damage, and Mac sent for Roger to handle the anaesthesia before giving instructions to the nurses about the instruments and sutures he'd need.

It took three hours, but eventually the young man had what looked like a patchwork but recognisable foot.

'I'd like to keep him here for his parents' sake,' Mac said, turning his attention to Izzy, one professional to another. 'He'll need strong IV antibiotics and at least twenty-four hours of intensive care to monitor him. Can we handle that?'

She knew he'd asked because it was a nursing question and as nurse manager it would be her decision.

'Yes,' she said, no hesitation. 'We'll have to juggle rosters but we can have someone with him for twenty-four hours, and you can review things after that.'

'Good,' he said, nodding at her, although a little frown that she knew had nothing to do with Ahmed now creased his brow.

'I'll sort out the rosters,' she said. 'Abby, will you take the first shift?'

She left the room, not needing a reply, and not wanting to spend any more time with Mac now the emergency situation was easing and it would be harder to pretend they were nothing more than colleagues.

Though perhaps after her behaviour last night, he'd be pleased to return to just being colleagues, perhaps thinking he'd had a lucky escape...

Izzy covered Abby's shift, knowing it was Sod's Law that they had an unusual number of ED visitors, a small boy with a fish hook in his foot, needing Mac to cut it out and stitch it up;

a pregnant woman complaining of feeling sick, her blood pressure far too high, protein in her urine test, all signs of pre-eclampsia.

'Do you usually admit a pre-eclampsia patient for bed rest?' Mac asked Izzy.

'When the blood pressure is this high, we do,' she said. 'We can monitor the baby's well-being as well as hers.'

'I'll give her a series of magnesium sulphate injections—latest studies seem to indicate it can stop it developing to full-blown eclampsia.'

Izzy sent an aide to organise a bed, and prepared the first of the injections Mac wanted while he talked quietly to the patient, explaining what was happening in her body, why it sometimes happened, and how resting and the medication could help her through the pregnancy.

'But the other kids?' she wailed, as Mac gave her the injection.

He looked helplessly at Izzy.

'Three,' she said, 'one at school, two still at home with Mum.'

She turned her attention to their patient.

'Where are the children now?' she asked.

'Their dad's with them but he's back to work tomorrow.'

Izzy touched her lightly on the shoulder.

'Don't worry. I'll talk to Hallie, she'll organise something then go and see your husband and explain it all to him.'

The woman looked relieved, but Mac was obviously puzzled.

'Does Hallie run the entire town?' he asked, and their patient smiled.

'Just about,' she said, 'and if it comes to organising things she's the best so I know whatever she does for the kids, they'll be okay.'

'What *does* she do in cases like this?' Mac asked Izzy as the patient was wheeled away.

Unable to look directly at him, Izzy busied herself cleaning up the room.

'There are a lot of groups—Country Women's Association, church groups, Girl Guides—they all have people who love to volunteer. You'll find she'll soon have a roster of babysitters and probably a cook and a gardener as well, making sure the family is well cared for.'

Mac nodded slowly.

'I suppose to some extent the army is the same, only there it would be a welfare officer organising it all. And possibly not as efficiently. She'd have made general in the army, your Hallie.'

And Izzy couldn't help but smile at the compliment, but smiling at Mac reminded her of all the reasons she shouldn't, reminded her of all the stuff she had to sort out before she could talk to him—or Nikki for that matter.

Just the thought of it made her feel ill.

'I'd better get on to the general, then,' she said, and slipped away, the ED suddenly quiet, and therefore a dangerous place to be with Mac…

Mac drifted through the hospital, physically there and doing his job, but a part of his mind still struggled with the truly weird experience he'd had the previous evening, when Izzy had gone from a lively and generous lover to a—

Madwoman?

Was she bipolar?

Had some other personality disorder?

But why would his name have triggered such an extreme reaction—so extreme she'd momentarily forgotten they were in her house, not his?

His heart felt heavy with…

What?

Love unspoken?

Despair that whatever it had been between them was now over?

No, there had to be a rational explanation. It was just a matter of getting some time alone with her, and the two of them talking.

Sensibly, rationally.

But he remembered the feel of her skin against his, heard the little noises she'd made as she'd writhed on the bed beneath him.

Could he really be rational about this when just thinking of the previous night had him hard?

At work?

What had happened to common sense?

Professionalism?

He grabbed a roomy white coat from the laundry, although he rarely wore one on the wards, and did a round, not seeing her, but checking all their patients.

He had notes to write up about the district meeting, figures to get ready for the district director, plenty of work to keep him in his office *and* to block a certain red-haired nurse completely from his mind.

Not easy when Hallie arrived, wanting a bit of information about how long he expected the woman with pre-eclampsia to be in hospital.

'Just so I have some idea of how long she'll need help, although she'll still need someone to lend a hand when she gets out, won't she?'

Mac told her what he thought, agreed she'd need help even when he let her go.

'It will depend on whether her blood pressure comes down and stays down,' he explained. 'If not, I'll keep her in until the baby's due. If it goes into full eclampsia—'

'She'll need a Caesar,' Hallie finished for him. 'I started nursing here in the days when the doctors did the lot—well, doctors and nurses—we had a great midwife.'

Mac had to smile. This woman took everything in her stride—much like Izzy, he supposed, although he didn't really know, Izzy, did he?

Had it all been just too sudden?

Was that what lay behind the panic?

'Are you settling in?' Hallie asked, and he hoped she couldn't read what he'd been thinking on his face.

'Yes, fine, thank you.'

She laughed!

'That's far too polite given you've had one crisis after another from the moment you arrived. I hope Izzy's been some help. She's got a good head on her shoulders, that one. I sometimes think of all the children I've had over the years, she's—well, parents shouldn't have favourites—but Izzy's close. Lila, of course, is Pop's little gift from God. He saved her, you know, from a burning car and she's clung to him ever since.'

And, having delivered these scraps of information, Hallie departed, off to organise her army of volunteers, small-town spirit at its best.

Which was when he realised he *was* settling in, beginning to see how small towns worked...

Feeling at home here?

Well, he *had* been...

Izzy shuffled the nursing rosters, phoned around to see who was available, then drew up a list of those who'd special Ahmed, checking for symptoms of delayed shock or infection, looking after his parents who were taking turns beside his bed.

She put herself down for Ahmed duty for the night shift—doing double shifts had never worried her—but now she'd sneak off home and have a sleep before she began her regular shift at two.

Sneak off?

Well, not exactly, although she crossed her fingers that she wouldn't see Mac as she made her escape.

Crossing fingers—what a childish thing to

do—but somehow that was how she felt: as bewildered as she'd sometimes been as a child, having to make a decision that seemed far too complex for her brain.

More than one decision…

Of course she could ignore it—say nothing?

Not to Nikki—

Not to Mac—

And be haunted for the rest of her life?

Once safely home she showered again, feeling new sensitivity in her body, thinking of Mac's hands, his kisses, the joy she'd been feeling.

But she had to sleep, so in the end put all thoughts and memories resolutely from her mind and did sleep, waking just in time to change into a uniform, make a sandwich to eat on the walk down the hill, and arrive at work on time.

She'd just grabbed a sticky bun from the kitchen and was heading for the nurses' station for handover when she ran into Mac.

Inevitably ran into Mac!

'I saw you've put yourself down for the night

shift, specialling Ahmed,' he said, very colleague-to-colleague, pure professional.

Well, she could do professional—or would
have been able to if she couldn't feel the bit of
pink icing from the bun on her cheek.

'I don't mind doing a double shift. And if he's
restless, it's better for him to have someone he
knows with him rather than one of the agency
nurses we have available. He's been trying to
teach me to surf—not having much success, but
we have a laugh together.'

She wanted to swipe her finger across her
cheek, but didn't want to draw attention to the
icing.

Some hope! It was Mac's finger that did the
swiping, Mac's finger that held up the tell-tale
smear before licking it, smiling, and saying, 'Delicious,' in a tone that made her cheeks burn.

Mac saw the colour rise beneath her skin,
waited, hoping she'd say something, hoping—

Well, he didn't know what he hoped, except
that he'd been keeping an eye on the back entrance to the hospital for the last ten minutes,

wanting to catch her, hoping perhaps they could talk.

But when he saw her, iced bun half-eaten in her hand, a smear of pink icing on her cheek, he'd had no words.

He'd lost the questions he wanted to ask—couldn't remember even the basic one—what had happened last night—

Now she whisked away, into the bathroom, no doubt to clean her sticky fingers and check for icing on her face.

How could she think of such mundane things when he burned to know what was going on between them?

When he wanted to know if there *was* anything between them?

Oh, for Pete's sake, what was he doing, maundering around like this?

He didn't do love, he reminded himself, he dallied, and if the initial meeting in a dalliance didn't work, he moved on.

So move on now!

Right now!

Phone Frances to apologise for leaving the barn dance early, find out whether he was keeping a three-legged goat fed for a year, maybe ask her over to try his Moroccan tagine, which he hadn't actually made just yet, still surviving on toast and packet soup, and a nourishing lunch the kitchen supervisor insisted he eat.

But he didn't phone Frances, instead he checked on Ahmed, talking to his gentle mother, calming down.

Ahmed's condition remained stable through the night, although Izzy was worried about the swelling in his foot. Had they missed a bit of foreign matter, or had infection set in? His temperature was a little raised, but otherwise he seemed to be sleeping peacefully, still dopey from the anaesthetic.

Her relief came in—it would be up to Mac or Roger, whoever was on duty later this morning, to decide if he still needed someone with him.

Weariness descended like a cloud, but aware the arguments going on in her head would keep her from sleep, she changed from her uniform to jogging clothes and set off along the path.

The physical exertion might help her sleep later, but it did little for the muddle in her mind. She tried to narrow it down, to decide what was the worst thing that could possibly happen, and knew the answer—losing Nikki—either Nikki's choice or Mac's, which brought her back to not telling…

Finally realising that after a double shift nothing was making any sense, she turned her attention to the world around her, seeing what looked like someone sitting by the fresh-water tap.

A walker coming from the other direction?

Another jogger, although now the mornings were getting colder not many were out this early.

By the time she was close enough to realise it was Mac, she was too close to him to suddenly turn tail and run.

Besides which, she had to talk to him sometime, if only to apologise for her behaviour the other night.

'Thought I might see you here,' he said, and

she tried desperately to hear something in his voice, or to see a clue as to what he was thinking in his eyes, his face.

'I need to apologise,' she said. 'I behaved stupidly. I'm sorry.'

'More panic than stupidity, I'd have thought.'

Still no hint of thoughts or feelings, while her own body was alive with sensation just being close to him.

Although maybe his coolness made things easier?

Perhaps he'd met to tell her it was all a mistake and they could forget what had happened and just be colleagues.

Except she couldn't forget—couldn't not tell—

'I'm sorry,' she said. 'Really sorry. You must have thought I was mad.'

He didn't answer, studying her instead, then a hint of a smile quirked one corner of his lips and her heart flipped in her chest.

'Not mad but definitely upset about something. Can you talk about it?'

If only he hadn't smiled. She sighed, and shook her head.

'Not just yet,' she said miserably. 'I really want to but I need to think it through, need to get *my* head around it before I can discuss it rationally.'

He reached out and took her hand, drew her closer, almost close enough to kiss, but no kiss, just his hand with a firm grip on hers.

'Maybe I can help,' he said quietly. 'I'm not a total idiot. I knew something I'd said, however inadvertently, had completely thrown you.'

He squeezed her fingers almost as if he didn't mind she'd been so weird.

'It took a while to make sense of it—in fact, it wasn't until last night I had time to actually sit down and go over the conversation we'd been having. And found no clues, until you asked my name.'

'Nicholas!' Izzy breathed the word.

'Nicholas indeed, and that's when I remembered! I'd been telling you about this girl—well, woman—I'd been seeing over in Bali, and when

I remembered telling you my first name I also remembered what she used to call me—'

'Nikki Mac?'

Izzy asked it as a question but she already knew the answer.

He nodded, face grave.

'Nikki?'

Izzy shrugged helplessly.

'I don't know—it's what I think. The whole time she was away her texts to me were of no one else—just Nikki Mac. I wanted details. Was it serious? "Not me, not ever!" she replied. It was just a lovely fling with a wonderful, intelligent man, and they both knew that was all it was. She went straight to Sydney to a job Steve had got for her—her dream job, she said.'

'Art,' Mac said, his voice dark, sober…

'She was brilliant,' Izzy remembered, brushing tears from her eyes. 'Drawing, painting, photography, she could make three lines on a piece of paper look like a scene, a few more and it would be a person.'

Mac stood up and drew her close enough to

put his arm around her shoulders, holding her, comforting her.

'I saw her work,' he said quietly. 'And she had such plans, such dreams.'

He let her go, turned away, staring out to sea.

'I killed them for her, didn't I? Carelessness on my part, her getting pregnant.'

Now Izzy went to him, touched his shoulder, moved closer.

'We don't know for sure, Mac. Health issues meant she was never regular, so I doubt she knew or even suspected for quite a few months. She knew she'd have support from all of us, but I think the tortured memories of her own childhood came back to haunt her when she realised she was pregnant, and it never took very much to turn Liane back to drugs. It was the only escape she knew and the slightest blip in her life would have her reaching for their oblivion.'

'I had to leave early. I should have found her, I should have checked she was okay.' Mac's own demons were now haunting him. 'She'd talked of Wetherby—that's where I heard the name—

but had told me she was going back to Sydney. Told me she was sterile, but still I should have checked. My father was ill, and I'd been posted to Townsville to begin my intern year. I thought about her often, but—'

'You weren't to know. Liane had told the truth as she knew it. She *had* been told she'd never have a child—her body too damaged in child-hood, and long-term drug use on top of that.'

Mac knew Izzy's words were meant to com-fort him, but the wound went too deep.

How could he not have found her?

How could he not have known he had a child?

How careless he had been back in those joy-ous holiday days, revelling in the magic that was Bali, and the beautiful woman who called him Nikki Mac?

He took a deep breath and turned back to Izzy. 'Nikki?' he said.

Izzy shook her head.

'I'm not up to that yet. I haven't worked it out. It frightens me, Mac—all the ifs and buts and maybes. I can't talk about it yet.'

She hesitated, then added, 'And in spite of the name and Nikki's blue eyes, she might not be your child. Wouldn't you want to be sure?

Mac knew the words made sense—of course they should make sure—but he also felt as if the night—and all his thinking—had given him something precious. A child...

Did he want to risk losing that?

'I'd be happy to accept her as mine. We could get married,' he said, trying hard to sound sensible and practical when inside he was a gibbering mess. 'Wouldn't that solve all the problems?'

'Get married?'

She almost yelled the words at him. '*You* don't want to get married, and *I* don't want to marry someone who isn't a for-ever-and-ever person, and how would Nikki feel? She's not stupid. She'd know we were doing it for her and that would be a terrible burden for her to bear.'

'It was just a thought,' Mac said, slightly staggered that she'd been so adamant. He'd thought it quite a good idea. In fact, the more it moved around in his head now, the better it got.

Which just went to show how little he understood women, he supposed, although now the
thought was there it wasn't going to go away.

Marrying Izzy had become a very attractive
proposition...

All he had to do was work out how to do it—
how to persuade her...

Start with a kiss?

CHAPTER ELEVEN

IZZY MOVED AWAY, totally befuddled—by the conversation, by her body's traitorous reaction to Mac's closeness, and by the ridiculous proposal.

Possibly the ridiculous proposal should have come first.

'I'm going back,' she said. 'I need to run, to clear my head.'

And she set off at a brisk jog, pausing only to turn back.

'We should check,' she said. 'Steve had Nikki's DNA taken when she was a baby, wanting to be sure the sleaze bag Liane hooked up with for drugs wasn't the father. If I get a copy to you, can you ask someone to compare them?'

Mac frowned at her.

Had he been serious when he'd said testing

didn't matter—that he was happy to accept Nikki as his child?

'Well, could you?' she demanded, as tiredness, confusion and being close to him combined to make standing there any longer almost impossible.

He nodded, nothing more, and she jogged away, turning back a second time.

'You won't say anything to anyone?'

She'd meant to sound firm, in control, but knew it had come out as a wimpy, pathetic plea.

'As if I would,' Mac muttered at her, and she turned back to her run, racing now, as if demons snapped at her heels.

She had to talk it through with someone, try to get her head around it all.

Hallie would be the ideal listener, and would probably offer sage advice, but to tell her about Mac's business—well, about his part in it, if he'd had a part in it—when she'd asked him not to say anything…?

She'd sleep on it, then maybe talk to Mac

again, be sensible about the test, so they could decide together how to go forward with it.

But being within a two-metre radius of Mac— forget that, being in the same postcode as him— caused so many physical reactions that battling them left little brain space for common-sense discussions.

Except she'd have to do it.

Maybe after a sleep she'd feel better, think better...

Mac walked slowly back to town, still taking in the fact he was a father, maybe, still obsessing that he should have done something earlier, kept in touch with Liane for all she'd kept reminding him that it would only ever be a holiday fling— a dalliance.

Had she used that word?

Was that where he'd picked it up?

Surely not! He'd moved on, worked, met and married Lauren, been divorced and worked some more.

Then Izzy!

He sighed and walked up to the hospital. Roger was on duty but Mac wanted to see Ahmed, and check on Rhia, *and* the pregnant woman they'd admitted with pre-eclampsia. For some reason seeing her safely through the rest of her pregnancy was suddenly very important.

Because he was a father?

Might be a father?

Nonsense!

Anyway, being a father was far more than the accident of conception. Being a father was a whole new world of learning.

He stopped at the bottom of the ramp leading into the hospital and turned to look out at the ocean, the revelation so strong it had stolen his breath.

It was what he wanted!

He wanted to be a father, to learn to be a father to Nikki—at least Nikki first. Somehow he and Izzy had to sort this out.

And he and Nikki?

Izzy was right, he had to compare their DNAs,

to know for certain, for Nikki's sake as much as his.

He turned back towards the hospital, the exhilaration of his revelation leaving a far more frightening question in his head.

What if Nikki didn't want a father—or want him as a father?

Hell's teeth, no wonder Izzy was in a muddle…

Sleep brought no answers for Izzy, if anything it made her feel more woolly-headed than ever. She made a cup of tea and stared at her much-changed roster on the door of the refrigerator. Next to it was Nikki's monthly calendar of the school and social events.

Rehearsals seemed to figure large in after-school activities for Nikki and it took a moment for Izzy to recall they must be coming up to the school concert. This was Nikki's first year in the high-school concert, held every second year, the primary school having a similar event in between.

But what was Nikki's group doing? A music video? Well, an onstage performance of a music video, all the year seven students involved either singing and dancing on stage, or making and shifting props around.

Nikki was singing, but then she always did, right from her first year at school.

Could Mac sing?

The thought stopped Izzy dead.

She *had* to do something and do it now!

Not right now as she had to go to work, but today, or tomorrow.

But right now she could contact Steve, get him to email a copy of the DNA results. Until they knew for sure, there was no point in upsetting Nikki with all of this.

But once they knew?

'Oh, help!'

She hadn't realised she'd said the words aloud until Hallie walked in, a tin of freshly baked biscuits in her hands.

'Help what?' Hallie demanded. 'I did knock

and when you didn't answer, I thought you'd gone to work.'

'On my way,' Izzy said, grabbing a couple of biscuits.

'And the help?' Hallie asked gently.

'Oh, Hallie, I don't know if anyone can help.'

And with that she departed.

Although maybe Mac and she could talk to Hallie together. Her mother had seen the best and worst that people could do to each other, and had wisdom that Izzy could never hope to acquire. And Hallie knew children, and relationships, and a lot of psychology...

Fortunately Mac wasn't at the hospital when she arrived, having gone in the ambulance to Braxton with the pre-eclampsia patient whose blood pressure had failed to stabilise and who would probably need a Caesar.

But tomorrow Mac was off, Nikki had early rehearsals, she'd ask Hallie to have a late breakfast with her and Mac in the flat, make pancakes—

She got that far in the planning before panic

set in so maybe that was a good thing. The panic usually came much earlier in her plans.

Mac returned as she finished giving out evening medications and the hospital was quietening down for the night.

'We should have DNA results in a couple of days. I forwarded that copy you emailed me of Nikki's along with mine—I had mine done when I joined the army—to a mate who'll fast-track it.'

The couple of days turned into a week, a week of sleepless nights and tortured days as far as Izzy was concerned. Her mind refused to function when it came to anything personal—Nikki, her, Mac—so she changed the hospital rosters yet again, putting herself on night duty to avoid at least one of the problems as much as possible.

But eventually the results came back, positive as she'd been sure they would be, and another weekend lay before them.

'It's Nikki we have to think about,' Mac said, slipping into a chair across the desk where she was writing up the night report, sliding the confirmation email across the desk towards her.

Izzy looked up at the man she'd been avoiding so assiduously, into the clear blue eyes, and felt her heart weep.

'I know,' she whispered. 'And it terrifies me!'

'Should we find someone to talk to first—a child psychologist?' Mac suggested, and Izzy realised he was as anxious about Nikki as she was.

'I was thinking Hallie,' she said. 'If anyone knows children, it's her. And Pop of course, but he's not one for words, but I thought if we talked to Hallie…'

Mac reached out and took her hand, squeezing her fingers gently.

'We'll work it out,' he said.

She gave a little huff that was half despair, half laughter.

'Will we?'

Mac left her to finish her shift, walking downtown to the promenade where he sat, looking out to sea, soothed by the sound of the surf.

And the answer came to him, so suddenly he

was suspicious of it. He turned it this way and that, studying it from all directions, from his, Nikki's and Izzy's points of view and decided, yes, he was right.

Excited now, he hurried back to the hospital to catch Izzy as she came off duty.

'Walk you home?' he said, and whether it was the lightness of his words, or the smile that followed them, Izzy stopped dead and stared at him.

'What is it?' she demanded. 'You've won lotto?'

He shook his head and took her hand.

'No, far better. I've thought of how to do it.'

He probably shouldn't have taken her hand as it had set all the nerves in his body atwitch, registering this was Izzy he was touching, reminding him just how attracted to her he was.

But he held tight and they walked together up the hill, bodies touching, hers bombarding his with silent messages that almost made him forget the purpose of the walk.

'You've thought of how to do it?' she finally

prompted, no doubt battling her own awareness of him.

Remembering them naked together, as he'd been?

'*I'll* talk to Nikki,' he announced, then wondered why this brilliant solution didn't seem to have affected Izzy as much as he'd thought it would.

'Why? What about?'

He stopped, turned to face her, and took her face between his palms so he could look into her dark eyes, run his thumb across her soft lips.

'I'll talk to her about Liane, about our holiday together, tell her about the Liane I knew, explain why we parted—different life paths for each of us—and how I didn't know about the pregnancy, didn't know I had a child, a daughter.'

He felt the smile as her cheeks moved in his hands.

'And then?'

He dropped his hands and drew her close, slipping his arms around her to hold her loosely in front of him.

'I haven't quite got that far, but she'll have stuff to say, questions, opinions. I thought we'd take a walk, maybe to the lighthouse, and you'd come, too, but be a bit apart, but she'll need you, I know she will.'

He leaned forward and kissed her lightly on the lips.

'What do you think?'

How could she think?

Standing here so close to Mac, his words whirling in her head while emotion whirled in her body.

Instinctively, it felt right what he'd said, or what she'd understood of what he'd said.

And outside, walking, that was good, less formal and more relaxed.

Well, Nikki might be relaxed, at least to start with, but Izzy could feel tension building in her body just thinking about the situation.

She leaned into Mac, and his arms tightened about her.

'We'll work it out, you'll see,' he said, and he sounded so convinced she almost believed him.

Almost because even fuzzy-headed, she could imagine so many scenarios that wouldn't be right—

Or was she over-thinking?

Mac was rubbing his hands up and down her arms, warming and reassuring at once.

'It will be a start,' he finally said. 'We both know this will be a huge emotional mess to dump on Nikki, but together, all three of us, I'm sure we can work through it.'

Izzy nodded, wanting nothing more than to stay there in his arms—for the moment to continue for ever.

'Go get some sleep,' Mac whispered. 'We'll talk later, maybe go out, the three of us, tomorrow afternoon.'

And maybe tomorrow wouldn't come…

But tomorrow did come, and the rush to get Nikki off to another rehearsal with the necessary props meant there was little time for explanations, although Izzy did mention Mac had asked if they'd both like to walk up to the lighthouse with him later in the day.

'Can Shan come?'

Izzy shook her head. She should have expected the question. Since the pair had first met in primary school, Shan had been included in most of their excursions, trips and even holidays.

'Not today.'

Izzy hoped her tone was light enough for Nikki not to ask the inevitable why, but apparently Nikki had already put her own interpretation on the outing.

'Is he going to ask my permission to marry you?' Nikki teased, and Izzy chased her out the door.

But he *had* asked, Izzy remembered, only because of Nikki and family, though, not because he loved her.

Before the thought could settle in her heart, she got busy, doing the spring clean she'd been promising to do, decluttering and cleaning the little flat with ferocious energy.

Anything to stop her thinking about what lay ahead.

About Nikki and how she would take it, what

it would mean to her, and the big one—where did they all go from there...?

Mac had arranged to meet them at three, and with no little trepidation Izzy walked with Nikki down to his house.

'I thought we'd drive to the parking area at the bottom of the hill,' he said, stowing a backpack into the boot of the car.

'Is that food?' Nikki asked, and Mac laughed.

'Food and drink—all kinds of stuff that's bad for you, like chips, and cake, and soft drink.'

'So we'll have a picnic, that's great. We haven't been up there for ages, have we, Mum?'

Which was when Izzy realised that her nerves were so taut she was beyond even the simplest conversation. She made a noise she hoped would be taken for agreement and climbed into the car, where Mac's presence was nearly as overwhelming as her tension.

But once walking up through the coastal scrub towards the top of the hill, she relaxed. Mac, with his loaded backpack, was walking with

Nikki, asking her about the concert, about her singing, whether she enjoyed it.

Seeing the two of them together, there was no way Izzy couldn't ask herself about what might have been, although she knew it was time to look to the future, not dwell on the past.

But a tear for Liane slid down her cheek.

Finding a sheltered spot where they'd be out of the wind but still able to look out at the ocean, Mac spread the picnic blanket he'd purchased that morning, then brought out his goodies.

As they settled down, drinks in hand, Nikki raised her glass to him, grinned, and said, 'Well, if we're not here so you can ask my permission to marry Mum, why are we here?'

'Nikki!' Izzy protested, but Mac had to laugh. The cheeky question had broken the tension that had been building in him all day.

'No, I've already asked her that and she didn't think it a good idea, but this *is* a family thing, Nikki, and something that's hard for me to tell and maybe going to be even harder for you to hear. I want to talk to you about Liane, your birth mother. You see, I knew her once, a long time ago.'

'You *knew* Liane! But that's amazing, and it's not hard to hear at all. I'm always asking the family about her, poor woman. What chance did she have after such an appalling childhood? And even when she came to live with Hallie she was never happy—running away, getting into trouble, on and off drugs.'

'Exactly,' Mac said, 'but I didn't know about that—she never talked about it—never mentioned the past at all. We were both on holiday, I'd just finished at university and she—well, Izzy tells me Liane had been in detox and the holiday was her reward for being off the drugs.'

'Was this in Bali?'

Mac hesitated. Somehow Nikki was leaping ahead of all his carefully prepared sentences. Had she already guessed where this was going? He looked at Izzy who was looking steadfastly out to sea—no help at all.

'It was,' he told Nikki, and he took her hand.

'And it was magical! The beautiful place, the smiling people, the beaches and the surf, we had such fun. We went up into the mountains, climbing to the very top of a peak that looked out over all the island, we wandered around temples where monkeys played, and bought flowers to weave in Liane's hair—hair like yours, that golden-brown colour.'

He paused, uncertain how this was going, Nikki's eager face suggesting she was taking it all in.

'Go on,' she whispered, so he did.

'She was special, your mother. She laughed and sang—that must be where you get it—and everywhere she went people smiled at her. She was like a beautiful bird or a brilliant butterfly, you had to look at her all the time, to watch her for the extra shine she seemed to bring to everything around her.'

He hesitated, but then added, 'And I loved her.'

Nikki was sitting very still, Izzy apparently turned to stone, but once he'd started, he knew he had to keep going.

'The trouble was it was a holiday—two weeks—and at the end we both knew we'd be parting. I was in the army—they'd trained me as a doctor and I'd been posted to Townsville way up in North Queensland—and she had a fabulous job waiting for her in Sydney. So we'd told ourselves all along it was just for now, and living for the moment, for the day, probably what made it so special.'

He paused, remembering that fateful moment in the hotel.

'As it turned out, we didn't even get two weeks!' he said. 'Two days before our holiday finished I had a message from home. My father was seriously ill and I had to go home. The army gave me leave but it was weeks before he was out of danger, and by then I had to get to Townsville.'

'You didn't keep in touch, didn't email, text, even read each other's social media pages?'

Mac took a deep breath.

'We'd agreed not to, but leaving the way I did, I tried to get in contact with her, but it was as if she'd been nothing but a dream. When she didn't return my calls or emails, I understood she'd meant what she'd said but I cannot tell you how deeply I regret not persevering. I should have contacted her, if only to make sure she'd got to Sydney safely—but we'd promised not to spoil what we'd had by trying to make it last long distance.'

He took Nikki's other hand and waited until she looked up at him.

'I'm sure you've guessed where this is going, and I know this must be terribly hard for you, but I had no idea. Liane said she had been told by doctors that she could never have children. We lived and loved and laughed because we knew our time together was so limited. If I'd known, if I'd even suspected—but I didn't, and what happened happened, and I cannot say how sorry I am.'

The silence was so loud it hammered in Mac's ears as he waited for a reaction.

'So you're my dad?' Nikki said at last, studying his face as if she might recognise it. 'Are you sorry about that?'

'Good grief, no, it's the most amazing thing that's ever happened to me, apart from meeting Liane. Izzy worked it out kind of by accident, but we've checked and it's true. I'm still getting used to it and I don't know if I can be called a dad when you've gone all this time without me to do dad things with you, but I'd like to start, if that's okay with you, and maybe if we start small and get to know each other, eventually it will seem right to both of us.'

'You can walk me down the aisle when I get married!'

The remark was so unexpected that Mac could only gape, but Izzy burst out laughing and reached out to hug her daughter.

'Oh, Nikki, you do bring everything back to basics.'

She pushed the long golden-brown hair off Nikki's face and looked into her eyes.

'I know this is all a huge thing for you to take in. It's been pretty huge for Mac and me as well, but we'll both be there for you, to answer questions or talk about the situation. As Mac said, he can't become an instant father but I think he's a good man and he'll soon learn the job.'

'It's really weird,' Nikki responded, shaking her head as if that might help all the information settle. 'To think I've got a dad. Just wait till I tell Shan and the girls at school.'

And hearing that, Izzy relaxed, smiling at Mac across what was suddenly *their* daughter.

Silence fell between them, punctuated occasionally by a question or remark.

'You really loved her?' Nikki asked.

'I really did,' Mac said, with such conviction Izzy knew it was true.

More silence, then, 'Does this mean we can shift into the doctor's house with Mac? It's a great house, I've always loved it.'

'It does *not*,' Izzy said firmly.

'But you could come for sleepovers,' Mac replied.

'But if we moved in, then you and I would get to know each other better. You said we'd have to do that before we could love each other like a dad and daughter, and if we were living there you and Mum could grow to love each other, too, and then get married and we'd be a family.'

'Pushing things, Nikki!' Izzy warned, well aware of how the girl could tease, and embarrassed that Mac should be put in such a delicate position.

But she'd underestimated Mac.

'It's a great idea, but we needn't rush things,' he told Nikki. 'And I don't need your mother living in my house to fall in love with her because that's already happened.'

Izzy simply stared at him, her lips moving in protest but no sound coming out, and when they did come out they made no sense.

'You can't—you don't—that's silly—'

Nikki, however, was ignoring her, her gaze riveted on Mac.

'You're kidding me, right? You've come down here, found a daughter and fallen in love with her mother—that's fairy-tale stuff, not real life.'

Mac smiled.

'Sounds like it, doesn't it, but it wasn't entirely magical. I had some rough times in the army and needed somewhere peaceful, and I remembered Liane mentioning Wetherby, just once. It was a place, she said, where nothing ever happened. That was exactly what I was looking for so, really, it was your birth mother who brought me here and that's how I found you.'

'Shan will *never* believe this!'

Izzy smiled at Mac and said, 'It's okay, that's a normal reaction from a nearly thirteen-year-old. And I think the days of nothing ever happening in Wetherby are over—if you think Nikki's excited about talking to her friends, wait until the town gossips get hold of this.'

Mac groaned, but he was smiling, and somehow the awkwardness that had stopped the conversation with his love declaration was gone.

Fortunately!

Gone but not forgotten. They lingered on the hill until the sun began to sink over the rolling hills to the west, then packed up their picnic and walked back to the car.

'Can you drop me at the restaurant so I can tell Shan?' Nikki asked, excitement shimmering in her voice.

Mac looked at Izzy who shrugged, and said, 'Might as well get it over and done with,' she told him. 'The sooner the story starts on the rounds, the sooner it will die. But I need to go home and talk to Hallie and Pop before they hear it from someone else.'

'I'll come with you,' Mac said quietly, and Izzy groaned, but inwardly.

It was the right thing to do, but what she really needed was time away from him.

Not that she believed the love thing he'd said. How could he be in love with her, he who dallied rather than loved?

But having him with her to see Hallie and Pop was a good idea so she'd think about the love business later.

The couple she considered her parents were in the kitchen, sharing a rare bottle of wine.

'Good,' Hallie said, 'you can each have a glass.

Pop and I don't ever finish the bottle. It always seems like a nice idea but one glass does us.'

Izzy and Mac joined them at the kitchen table, accepted their wine from Pop, sipped and—

'Something you want to tell us?' Hallie asked.

'Yes, but it's more Nikki than us. Well, us in some ways, or more precisely Mac, but—'

'Perhaps you should let Mac tell us,' Pop said gently, moving his chair closer to Izzy and putting his arm around her shoulders.

So Mac did, leaving little out, explaining that they'd told Nikki, and she was already spreading the news.

'How did she take it?' Hallie asked, and Mac looked to Izzy to answer.

'Okay so far, but there'll be questions and it will take time for it all to sink in. It's not every day you find your father.'

'Nor every day a father finds his daughter either,' Hallie reminded her, looking at Mac with raised eyebrows.

'In truth, I'm lost,' he said, 'so many conflicting emotions churning inside me. Regret

I wasn't there for Liane, that I wasn't there for Nikki when she was born, then worry—or more probably terror—that I might not be any good at this dad business. And now I've found her, what if she decides she doesn't want me? Not immediately—there'll be novelty value for a while, I imagine—but down the track. What if she blames me for her mother going back onto drugs? For her mother's death?'

Hallie smiled and poured him another drink.

'Do you think all parents don't go through that list of doubts and many, many more, every day of their lives? You just hang in there, do your best, be yourself, be as truthful as you can, and hope it all works out.'

'You make it sound so easy,' he said, and Pop shook his head.

'We all know it's not, but worrying about what might be never got anyone anywhere. It's like the holiday you took with Liane, take each day as it comes and get as much joy as you can from it. That's how Hallie and I always worked. Yes, there'll be tears and probably tantrums and you'll do or say the wrong thing, but with love, and patience, things usually come right at the end.'

Having made a speech far longer than she could remember ever hearing from Pop, Izzy was surprised when he turned to her.

'Are you all right with all of this, lass?' he asked, and Izzy felt tears prick at her eyelids.

'Just about,' she admitted. 'Though it will take time for all of us. I think it's the most wonderful thing for Nikki and, really, that's all that matters.'

'Humph!' Pop said. 'That's the way you always think, but it's time you put yourself first, Izzy. Think of what *you* want and how you would like this to work for you.'

'Pop's right,' Hallie put in, and Izzy held up her hands in surrender.

'Okay, but like we've all been saying it'll take time. It's a big change in all our lives, a huge change for Nikki and Mac—so we all need time to work out where we fit.'

And suddenly the energy that expectation and

concern had built in her all day drained away, leaving her in a state of total exhaustion.

'In fact, if you'll all excuse me, I really need to have a hot shower and a wee rest before I can even begin to think about the future.'

Mac was on his feet immediately.

'I'll walk you up to the flat,' he said, but Hallie held up her hand.

'Let her go, Mac,' she said gently. 'It's been a lot for her to handle as well, and do you think she doesn't have a list of doubts and what-ifs as long as yours?'

Mac subsided into his chair once more, and Izzy beat a hasty retreat.

Her mind was blank—overloaded, she knew—and much as she'd have liked to have Mac's arms around her, she was so emotional she knew where it would lead.

Which was another complication she'd think about later, along with that strange declaration.

How could he love her when he didn't do love?

CHAPTER TWELVE

HE WAS WAITING at the fresh-water tap again the next morning, appearing like a wraith in the light sea mist.

'So, shall we get married?' he said as she bent over to catch her breath.

Catch her breath when he'd just made what sounded very like an extremely casual but probably serious proposal?

She straightened cautiously, and looked into the now-familiar blue eyes.

'Why?' she asked.

He kind of smiled and kind of shrugged, and reached out to touch her cheek.

'It just seems like a good idea,' he finally replied, no smile now, deadly serious.

'For you, for Nikki, or for me?' Izzy asked, the

hammering of her heart against her sternum telling her just how important his answer would be.

Wishing...

Hoping...

'For all of us,' he said.

Wrong answer!

Her head dropped, her eyes watered, her body trembled in reaction and he reached out and put his hands on her shoulders, drawing her slightly closer but not close enough for body contact.

Just close!

'And...' he said, and she could read stress in his face, feel tension in his hands.

'And...' she prompted.

Wrong prompt!

'Damn it, Izzy, you know why. I told you yesterday that I love you.'

'You told Nikki that you love me,' Izzy reminded him gently, although her heart had stopped hammering and was doing a little skipping thing in her chest. 'Not the same thing.'

'But you heard me say it,' he protested, and she wondered if she should give him a break.

No way!

'Not to me!'

He drew her close, clasped his arms around her back and rested his chin on her head.

'Oh, Izzy, I have no idea why it's so hard. Perhaps because I've thought for a long time that people say it too readily, too often, and the words lose their meaning. But I've known for days now, probably weeks, yet putting how I feel into words—'

'You're doing okay,' Izzy whispered, feeling the love through the lips in her hair, the hands on her back.

'I love you, Izzy. There, I've said it, but it wasn't just words, it was a pledge of my heart, my life, my love for ever. All for you, my for-ever-and-ever woman!'

She raised her head to his for the kiss to seal the declaration, but put her finger to his lips before they touched hers.

'Isn't it my turn now?' she asked, then had to laugh at the astonished look on his face.

'But of course you love me,' he said. 'You

must! We're meant to be together. Even without Nikki it would have been you and me. Besides, you have to marry me, because being with you, loving you has stopped my nightmares.'

'Well, there's a good reason,' Izzy teased.

But Mac was serious again.

'Not as good as love,' he said quietly. 'I think we both knew there was something special between us from our first meeting at the beach that morning. It was as if a whole new world had started—for me anyway.'

'For me, too,' Izzy agreed, and now she did kiss him, revelling in the sense of belonging that filled every cell in her body.

'I love you, Mac,' she whispered as they pulled apart.

'And I you,' he confirmed, and he took her hand to walk back along the track—to a daughter, to marriage, to a family…and to happy ever after.

* * * * *

*If you enjoyed this story,
check out these other great reads
from Meredith Webber:*

*A SHEIKH TO CAPTURE HER HEART
THE MAN SHE COULD NEVER FORGET
THE ONE MAN TO HEAL HER
THE SHEIKH DOCTOR'S BRIDE*

All available now!

MILLS & BOON®
Large Print Medical

September

Their Secret Royal Baby	Carol Marinelli
Her Hot Highland Doc	Annie O'Neil
His Pregnant Royal Bride	Amy Ruttan
Baby Surprise for the Doctor Prince	Robin Gianna
Resisting Her Army Doc Rival	Sue MacKay
A Month to Marry the Midwife	Fiona McArthur

October

Their One Night Baby	Carol Marinelli
Forbidden to the Playboy Surgeon	Fiona Lowe
A Mother to Make a Family	Emily Forbes
The Nurse's Baby Secret	Janice Lynn
The Boss Who Stole Her Heart	Jennifer Taylor
Reunited by Their Pregnancy Surprise	Louisa Heaton

November

Mummy, Nurse...Duchess?	Kate Hardy
Falling for the Foster Mum	Karin Baine
The Doctor and the Princess	Scarlet Wilson
Miracle for the Neurosurgeon	Lynne Marshall
English Rose for the Sicilian Doc	Annie Claydon
Engaged to the Doctor Sheikh	Meredith Webber

MILLS & BOON®
Large Print Medical

December

Healing the Sheikh's Heart	Annie O'Neil
A Life-Saving Reunion	Alison Roberts
The Surgeon's Cinderella	Susan Carlisle
Saved by Doctor Dreamy	Dianne Drake
Pregnant with the Boss's Baby	Sue MacKay
Reunited with His Runaway Doc	Lucy Clark

January

The Surrogate's Unexpected Miracle	Alison Roberts
Convenient Marriage, Surprise Twins	Amy Ruttan
The Doctor's Secret Son	Janice Lynn
Reforming the Playboy	Karin Baine
Their Double Baby Gift	Louisa Heaton
Saving Baby Amy	Annie Claydon

February

Tempted by the Bridesmaid	Annie O'Neil
Claiming His Pregnant Princess	Annie O'Neil
A Miracle for the Baby Doctor	Meredith Webber
Stolen Kisses with Her Boss	Susan Carlisle
Encounter with a Commanding Officer	Charlotte Hawkes
Rebel Doc on Her Doorstep	Lucy Ryder

0817 LP 2P P2 Medical

MILLS & BOON®
Large Print – September 2017

ROMANCE

The Sheikh's Bought Wife	Sharon Kendrick
The Innocent's Shameful Secret	Sara Craven
The Magnate's Tempestuous Marriage	Miranda Lee
The Forced Bride of Alazar	Kate Hewitt
Bound by the Sultan's Baby	Carol Marinelli
Blackmailed Down the Aisle	Louise Fuller
Di Marcello's Secret Son	Rachael Thomas
Conveniently Wed to the Greek	Kandy Shepherd
His Shy Cinderella	Kate Hardy
Falling for the Rebel Princess	Ellie Darkins
Claimed by the Wealthy Magnate	Nina Milne

HISTORICAL

The Secret Marriage Pact	Georgie Lee
A Warriner to Protect Her	Virginia Heath
Claiming His Defiant Miss	Bronwyn Scott
Rumours at Court (Rumors at Court)	Blythe Gifford
The Duke's Unexpected Bride	Lara Temple

MEDICAL

Their Secret Royal Baby	Carol Marinelli
Her Hot Highland Doc	Annie O'Neil
His Pregnant Royal Bride	Amy Ruttan
Baby Surprise for the Doctor Prince	Robin Gianna
Resisting Her Army Doc Rival	Sue MacKay
A Month to Marry the Midwife	Fiona McArthur

0817 GEN STD LP

MILLS & BOON®

Why shop at millsandboon.co.uk?

Each year, thousands of romance readers find their perfect read at millsandboon.co.uk. That's because we're passionate about bringing you the very best romantic fiction. Here are some of the advantages of shopping at www.millsandboon.co.uk:

* **Get new books first**—you'll be able to buy your favourite books one month before they hit the shops

* **Get exclusive discounts**—you'll also be able to buy our specially created monthly collections, with up to 50% off the RRP

* **Find your favourite authors**—latest news, interviews and new releases for all your favourite authors and series on our website, plus ideas for what to try next

* **Join in**—once you've bought your favourite books, don't forget to register with us to rate, review and join in the discussions

Visit **www.millsandboon.co.uk**
for all this and more today!